HIGH MOUNTAIN LOGGER

WALTER B. JOHNSON

iUniverse, Inc.
New York   Bloomington

High Mountain Logger

iUniverse books may be ordered through booksellers or by contacting:

iUniverse
1663 Liberty Drive
Bloomington, IN 47403
www.iuniverse.com
1-800-Authors (1-800-288-4677)

Because of the dynamic nature of the Internet, any Web addresses or links contained in this book may have changed since publication and may no longer be valid. The views expressed in this work are solely those of the author and do not necessarily reflect the views of the publisher, and the publisher hereby disclaims any responsibility for them.

ISBN: 978-1-4401-2788-5 (sc)
ISBN: 978-1-4401-2789-2 (ebook)

Printed in the United States of America

iUniverse rev. date: 6/12/2009

Chapter One
Sam's Story

Sam sat in the large, darkened, room filled with tables filled with people who were half drunk and talking loudly; the din was so loud because the large crowd had a hard time even getting the people, at their own tables, to hear them without raising their voices, and by they just being loud because they had been drinking. Beer signs surrounded the large wood paneled room, and a smoky haze floated from the crowded tables filling every nook and cranny of the club with the smoky smell. On the stage a Country band started playing loudly above the din. A girl with long blond hair, stacked high on her head, stood out front of the band, and with a high sweet voice sang a cheating country song. Sam sat with a full bottle of beer sitting in front of him surrounded by two or three more that were empty, and an ash tray full of cigarette butts. The slightly drunken feeling held him, that feeling that felt so good to him. It was too bad, once he felt that way he would often continue drinking and end up getting so drunk he had trouble walking. Now he wasn't completely drunk, he was in that twilight zone he always drank to enter. He was superman now and could not be touched by the world. He was confident and strong, and could tolerate the ego shattering denials thrown his way, so causally, by girls who didn't want to dance with him. He would tell himself the girl who had turned him down had made a big mistake and believe that it was her big loss, not his. It had taken him awhile to come up with that little mental trick, but it always helped him make it though his nights at the "Greenwood."

Sam was now twenty-five years old, married and a father of a young boy, and even though he believed he loved his family, there he was out dancing with the girls of the Greenwood. The fun two years that he spent in college had always remained with him. After his marriage seemed to have gone stale and boring to him, and not lived up to his romanticized notions, he was out again looking for those wild times. Now instead of being with a bunch of wild and crazy college students, he was alone except for his beer. There was loneliness to his nights at the "Greenwood," but there was also the thrill of the chase and sometimes his efforts were rewarded.

As the dancers were moving to the beat of the music, and all packed together with their serious expressions, Sam stared out on the dance floor sitting still as a stone. It was though he was in a trance as he watched the whirling, bouncing figures moving in the dark room. He was really enjoying the action, he always did, but eventually he pulled himself out of his trance, as a song ended, and began searching the room checking out the girls without partners.

Soon he picked out one that he thought fitted his tastes better than the rest, and he thought would be willing to dance with him. Slowly rising to his feet he walked over to her table, and bent down next to her and said softly, "Would you like to dance?" She turned her head, but said nothing then coolly rose to her feet slowly and started walking to the dance floor. Sam was right behind, watching her as she moved ahead of him. They stopped at the edge of the dance floor and began to dance. It was a fast dance so they danced a few feet apart, the girl not looking at him, but seeing him anyway. At first Sam concentrated on his dancing until he was at ease. Then he began looking at the girl, getting a good look at her for the first time. He liked what he saw, a very good looking girl who was a great dancer. He loved dancing with girls like her, but he had little luck getting to know girls as good looking as she was. "The "Greenwood" was a dance hall located in Springfield, Oregon. It was late autumn, 1970, when young Sam was patrolling the dance floors in Springfield and Eugene. Springfield was and is a blue collar town with many loggers and mill workers living there and they would fill the "Greenwood" to the brim on the weekends. Sam would make an excuse to his wife and drive the thirty miles to Spriingfield for a night out on the town, trying to relive the excitement of his younger years. Sam had dated a little in high school but much more in college. He felt that he was in love twice while in college, and what a glorious feeling young love had been to him. The dating and the chasing, and the heightened emotions of what he thought was true love made that time of his life so exciting. It didn't help his grades, but it made life a party for him. He felt that same way when dating his wife and early in his marriage. He felt he was truly in love with his wife and would never dream of cheating on her. He felt after awhile, though, that she couldn't love him as completely as he wanted her to. He let his pride get in the way and his love wane until he was able to rationalize his way into making those evening trips to the "Greenwood." Sam had entered his marriage with the same romantic notions that propelled his life. To Sam there was nothing but love ahead for them. He thought Brenda would be just right for him because he had given their marriage so much thought. What impressed Sam so much was that she seemed so feminine. She didn't seem to have an aggressive bone in her body, which made her seem vulnerable, but that was one of the things that appealed to him. He wanted to protect her from the world and provide a safe haven for her and their children.

Sam liked the fast country song they were dancing to, and the look of the pretty girl with the long black hair, and big eyes dancing in front him, so he soon said, "My name is Sam what is yours. She didn't answer him at first, but soon said after turning towards him causing him to almost run into her, and giving Sam a shock by staring into his eyes with her beautiful brown eyes as they stood almost nose to nose. "My name is Shannon." She then quickly turned and danced away to the beat of a twanging county guitar and the wailing of the soulful, country voice that filled the room. It was not a good sign for Sam, but he followed her trying to get close enough to talk to her. She soon turned and he was staring her in the face again making him more nervous than the already was. He could see a wry smile cross her face just as he said. "They have a great band tonight. Don't you think?" She just said, "Yes." and then danced away from him again, but this time as Sam followed the music stopped. Since Sam liked the music and looking at the girl dancing in front of him the music ended much too soon for him. He could tell by the way the pretty girl acted, though, that she wouldn't want to dance with him again, and then he knew for sure because without saying a word she quickly turned away from him and calmly walked back to her table without looking back leaving Sam standing their alone to trudge back to his table. He would have preferred to have danced a slow dance since he liked the feeling of holding a woman close to him. It was such a sensual pleasure for him. He would close his eyes and feel the softness of the girl's body as they moved slowly to the beat of the music, and he would always think that it felt so good that it had to be illegal. He would slowly drift into a trance holding her so close but so softly. Sometimes he would begin to have romantic notions about someone that he didn't even know. Somehow feeling that he was making a connedtion with the girl, and falling in love with her for the length of the dance, all that would end though when the music stopped, then the trance would be broken, and they would be strangers again as he walked the girl back to her table. However there were times, not very often, when he would find a girl who liked him and was willing to let him sit with her.

Later, as the night was winding down and many of the people who had been there when Sam first arrived were gone, Sam's attention was turned to the entrance. He always looked over when he noticed the door open hoping there would be an unescorted lady or ladies coming in to the "Greenwood". Sam knew what it was like to be at the "Greenwood" very late in the evening, because he would always stick around to enjoy the atmosphere until the last note was played. He was quickly running out of time if he was going to find a girl that night though. All the girls left at the "Greenwood" were taken, but to his great pleasure a man and two women walked thought the door. Sam knew that meant one of the girls was approachable, and one of the girls really caught his attention. She was wearing a blue denim coat and jeans and she was very well built which was something that always caught his attention. There was one thing that he knew of sure, right then and there, as he watched them walk in, that would really help him enjoy that night, and that was to dance with the girl in the blue denim coat. Sam thought she was a very good looking girl, not beautiful but very good looking. The kind of girl he felt that would be willing to dance with him. Even better the kind of girl that might even let him sit with her. The excitement quickly built in Sam as he sat at the edge of his seat waiting for another country tune to start. He wasn't going to let anyone beat him to her. The music started and Sam was off. In a few very quick steps he was asking her to dance. To his great pleasure she said "Yes." The first dance was a fast one. Sam, disappointed, hoped a slow one would follow so that he could hold her close. When the dance ended Sam quickly said, "Would you like to dance another one?" She looked at him and to his anxious ears said, "Okay." They stood at the edge of the dance floor waiting for the music to start, with Sam praying for a slow song. As they stood there without saying anything a little too long, Sam said to himself nervously, "Don't be a dummy, say something fast or she'll know you for the idiot you are!" So nervously, he said something he'd rehearsed, even though there wasn't much to it. "I've never seen you here before, are you from around here?" Although Sam was often at the "Greenwood" dancing with girls, and was sometimes lucky enough to sit with one and even leave with her, it was never easy for him. The drinking always helped his courage, though, as it did at that moment. The girl looked up at him, as they were now close enough for Sam to put his arm around her, and answered in what Sam thought was a friendly way, "I'm from Portland. I've been visiting my brother and his wife here in Springfield for the last month."

"You're from the big city! How do you like living in a small town like Springfield?"

"I like it here. I don't know anybody, but I've been enjoying myself." The music started again so they began to dance. To Sam's pleasure it was a slow one. Sam at first pulled her lightly to him, but then pulled back knowing that if he wanted to sit with her he had to keep talking so he asked. "What's you name? I'm Sam Jackson?"

"My name is Cheryl Peterson." Then she said, again in a friendly manner. "Do you live in Springfield?

"No, I live in a little town about thirty miles south of here, but they don't have anything like the "Greenwood". It's a quiet town with not much going on, especially on the weekends. They must have a lot going on in Portland as big as it is." Sam was motivated by his desire so the words cam easily and quickly as he continued. "I've always wanted to check out some of the places up there. I bet the clubs in Portland don't just play country music like they do around here."

"They have clubs that play country, rock. Jazz any kind of music you want. I don't go to the clubs very often though. Do you come here often?"

"Yea, I come here most weekends sometimes both Friday and Saturday." They had talked so little, but Sam thought they had conversed enough so that she wouldn't think that he was a complete dummy, and would invite him to sit with her. He wanted to hold her so badly he could not wait a second longer. So he gently pulled her close to him and enjoyed the rest of the dance with his eyes closed, lost in the sensations of Cheryl. The music ended too soon for Sam as he reluctantly let her go and watched her turn away from him and walk back to her table. He soon followed right behind her with a small smile creasing his face, showing the pleasure he had gotten from dancing with her. As soon as she got to her table and sat down, Sam leaned down beside her and said, "So you mind if I sit here with you?" Looking up at him she answered "No, I don't mind." When he sat down, she introduced him to the other two people at the table, her brother Danny and his wife Nancy. Sam was more than a little nervous, but he knew by then that he wanted to get to know Cheryl better, so he was going to try his hardest to make a good impression. Cheryl suddenly moved her big black purse, which was right beside her, and bent down searching under the table for something. Sam, smiling a little nervously, wondered what she was looking for. Her sister-in-law, sounding a little annoyed said, "Cheryl what are you doing?"

"I'm looking for my shoes." She then looked up at Sam and said. "I like to dance in my bare feet." Then she reached down into her big purse and started stirring her hand around inside it ample contents before bringing out a pair of blue rimmed glasses. "I don't like to wear my glasses when I go out, they look so ugly." When she put her glasses on she was able to quickly find her shoes and put them on. Everyone around the table, Including Sam, looked nervous for her while she struggled to find her shoes. Sam was beginning to feel that Cheryl didn't care much what anyone thought about what she did. He also knew that he wanted more than ever to get to know her. He broke the silence as he said." I think they have a great band tonight that is if you like country music." Danny looked away from watching the band and said. "I like the band to and we do like country music." Danny looked nothing like Cheryl he was rather short, stout, blond, blue eyed and looked strong enough for Sam to think that he must have been an athlete in high school. Cheryl was thin and tall for a girl, and he thought not athletic, but having what Sam thought was a very nice looking body. She had light brown hair, large hazel eyes, and a long face, and her straight hair ran to her shoulders, and closely, surrounded her face. A face, that Sam liked looking at. Just then Sam said, "This band plays here a lot." He looked at Danny and said, "Have you ever heard them play before?"

"Yes! We came here last week and they were playing then."

"Do you come here a lot?"

"No, I first came here with a friend of mine from work to drink a few beers during the week and found out they had a country band play here every weekend. Last weekend Sandy, Cheryl, and I came and liked it. We went to movies tonight, and as we drove by decided to stop and listen to the last few songs." Sam wanted very badly to talk to Cheryl and get to know her but Danny continued, "Do you live here in Springfield, Sam?"

"No, I live in a little town about thirty miles south of here called Crescent."

"I know Crescent; I drive by there on my way to Klamath Falls all the time. I'm a salesman and travel around the state selling medical equipment to hospitals. It seems like a nice little town. I've stopped there a couple of times for gas." Sam said, "Yea, It's all right we just don't have a place like the "Greenwood" down there, so on the weekends I drive up here." Danny, staring at Sam intently, asked, "What do you do for a living Sam?"

"I work in the woods. I'm a logger. I work for Roberts logging Company. Boney Roberts owns it. He's a Jippo Logger, or a small logger, who logs for Weyerhaeuser Lumber Company. We come all the way up here every morning during the week, and then drive up the Mackenzie River and up into the high Cascades to log." Cheryl broke in then, "May I interrrupt this interrogation. Sam, I'm sorry but my brother gets a little over protective of his little sister sometimes." Then she smiled at him and said, "He forgets I'm a big girl now." Sam thought she might be a little shy, but he could tell by her confident tone of voice and the way she broke into the conversation that she was not. The last song ended and they turned on all the lights signaling that it was time to leave. Danny said, as they were all blinking their eyes getting them used to the bright lights, "Well its nice meeting you Sam, but it looks like it is time to leave." Sam was worried that they would leave before he had a chance to ask Cheryl out so he quickly said, "Would you like to go with me on a date next weekend? We could go to the movies, or come here to dance if you like." She said without looking at him. "I'm going to Portland next weekend so I can't" Sam was unprepared for her abrupt manner, so said nothing. She did not say another word either, but sat down and started reaching into her big black bag as everyone else stood watching her. Sam felt he had been dismissed. It was obvious to him that she didn't want to see him again. This was something that he experienced more than a few times before so he knew the feeling well. Feeling disappointed, he started to turn and walk away. Just as he did, Cheryl pulled a small scrap of paper out of her purse and said to Sam's great relief, "Do you have a pen with you?" With a smile on his face, knowing why she wanted the pen, he said, sorry, no, I never carry one with me." He knew she must have wondered about his smile but he could not keep it off his face, especially with seeing her so upset that she could not find a pen. He was very anxious for her to find a pen also because he definitely did not want to lose her and was kicking himself for not having one. Cheryl started digging around in her purse again, seemingly very frustrated, and causing Sam to start feeling terrible as he was losing hope, but soon she pulled out what looked like a short pencil and held it up. "This eyeliner pencil should work." Sandy quickly spoke up, "Cheryl you can't write with that thing."

"It's all I have. I think it will work." Danny and Nancy stood around the table looking very anxious to leave as she wrote a number on the little scrap of paper. After she finished writing, Cheryl said, "It does work." She handed the little piece of paper to Sam, "This is my brother's phone number, and you can get in touch with me there most anytime. We have to leave now." Sam quickly said, "How about Sunday? Could we go out tomorrow?"

"Yes, I can go out tomorrow. Give me a call around two and let me know when you're coming over." Then she, her brother and his wife left Sam standing there alone. He watched them leave and then he left too feeling very good about the night as he drove home to Crescent and his family.

Chapter Two
The First Date

The next day Sam had not called by two o'clock. It was not that he did not want to call Cheryl, but being that he was usually shy, and often lacked confidence, when he was not half drunk, he kept procrastinating. At last at two that afternoon he said to his wife, since his brother did not have a phone. "Brenda, I'm going over to John's for awhile and help him work on his car. I should be back pretty early".

"Can't you stay home this evening? You were gone last evening."

"I owe John. He has helped me with my car a lot."

"Will you spend next weekend at home then?"

"Okay, next week will be yours, I promise." Sam then picked up his little boy and gave him a kiss on the cheek then left his family and started driving to Eugene. It's a city much larger than Springfield separated from it by the Willamette River. All the while that he drove through Crescent and to Eugene, and then through that city, he kept trying to get himself to call Cheryl. He passed phone booth after phone booth his fear, and lack of confidence, keeping him from stopping. One thing he knew though, and that was he wanted to see her and he wanted to see her badly, but he could not get over his shyness, and lack of confidence, He turned around after passing through Eugene and was ready to give up seeing Cheryl. He was ready to drive back home to his wife and his boy. He could see them all together in his mind and it felt very good to him. It helped his nervousness subside. He was not giving into his shyness he was doing what was right. He was going home and he was going to take his wife and little boy to the city park and be the father that he should be. He turned around and started driving back through Eugene on his way home to his family. As he drove on though, and came to the Springfield exit, his car slowly turned into the exit as if it had a mind of its own. Sam was not going home to his family; he was going to call Cheryl. She had won out over his family. Sam's resolve to go home to his family had disappeared as fast as it had appeared. His great desire to see Cheryl was controlling him and his anxiousness about calling her had waned. He stopped at the first public phone he came to and got out to make the call, but as he approached the phone the fear returned so he grabbed it decisively almost angrily, and dialed the number on the small piece of scrap paper he held in his hand. The voice on the phone was Cheryl's. He had hardly talked to her but he knew her voice, and for some reason the sound of her voice was calming on his nerves. So Sam calmly said, "Hello! This is Sam, the guy you met last night at the Greenwood." Cheryl answered, "Hi! How are you Sam?"

"Great," As he got right to the point because of his nervousness he said a little too quickly. "I was wondering if you would like to go out with me. There's a good movie playing at the Cascade Drive-Inn tonight." He did not have to wait long for an answer, as Cheryl answered quickly and spoke quickly. "I'm not doing anything tonight. Yes, I can go out with you." Sam's pulse quickened and his spirits soared, as he now knew he was going to see her for sure. Then he said, "Good I will pick you up at seven. How do I get to your house?"

"You drive down Gateway until you come to Spring Meadow then turn right for three blocks to Fifth Street, then left to the third house on the left, and that will be my brother's house. It will have a light blue station wagon sitting in front of it."

"Okay I got it. From Gateway I turn right on Spring Meadow for three blocks then turn left on Fifth Street, and your brothers house is the third one on the left, with the blue station wagon in front of it."

"If you can't find the house just call." He knew he would find the house, without calling her, as the directions were now etched in his brain. He answered her. "Alright I will see you at seven then."

"Bye Sam." Even though Cheryl had sounded so nice on the phone, and she agreed to go out with him, Sam was still glad the call was over. He knew that he would be uneasy until they were out on their date, and they had enough time to get comfortable with each other. He was sure that she would like him though once she got to know him. There were some girls he knew would never like him, but he did not believe that Cheryl was one of them.

It was only Four O'clock in the afternoon so he had a bunch of time to waste until he picked her up. He knew he shouldn't have started for Springfield so early knowing they would not be able to start the movie until after it got dark, but he had wanted to see her so badly. He also was almost broke so he would have just enough money to get them into the Drive-Inn and maybe buy a couple of cokes. He knew it was dumb for him to be trying to go out with Cheryl with him having so little money, but he decided he would take her out and hope that things would work out somehow. As Sam worried he passed the giant, tall, smoke stacks at the Weyerhaeuser Paper Mill spewing out their white smoke high into the sky. They dominated the Springfield sky line, and sometimes would put out a foul smell you could smell for miles. He didn't know how the people of Springfield could stand it. He didn't think he was going to back on the date, but he knew it would not be a sure thing until he knocked on her door at seven. He was driving his old beat up fifty six Ford. He had owned a nice looking five year Chevy Pick-Up, but the engine had blown up on him, so he was now driving his old ratty looking Ford that was heavily dented all along the passenger side, not enough to keep the doors from opening but bad enough. He had to put up with it until he could save enough for a down payment for something better. He could only hope that she would like him enough to overlook his old Ford. One of the impressions he had of her, though, was that she might be kind of a hippie. She wore her hair long and straight looking like so many of the hippie girls. If she were, he thought, she would not care about his ratty old Ford, and the fact that he could not take her to a nice place to eat, or even take out to eat at all. Weren't the hippies, he thought, supposed to be unpretentious and not care about material things? Thinking that made him feel a little better as he continued to drive through Springfield. He drove east far enough so that he left the city limits of Springfield and was out on the road that he and the logging crew took every morning of the week to get to where they were doing their logging. It was the road that ran along the cold, fast flowing Mackenzie River, and up and over the high Cascade Mountains. Sam knew exactly how cold and fast it could be. He had once gone down the river in a two-man rubber raft one very cold spring morning. He had floated down the river with Tommy, a high school friend. While he was in High School they held the White Water Parade every spring. River boats of every size and shape would float down the cold river with a crowd lining the shore. It was discontinued not long after Sam graduated because officials believed it had gotten too dangerous. The river was so cold that if the people who fell in didn't drown they would go into shock from the cold. Some people went down the river in special Mackenzie River Boats and they were very safe, and Sam's raft was safe enough although he and Tommy did have to bail icy water out of it as they floated down the river to keep it from sinking. The rafts made of truck and car inner tubes, tied together with rope were not so safe. They were often filled with wild and crazy college students and beer, and were the ones that were most likely to have someone fall into the river. The excitement of the parade was riding the white water rapids where the river turned into a wet roller coaster ride. The places, along the river, where Sam and Tommy would hold on tightly to the sides of the boat. As they were bounced and jerked around and splashed with the icy water. The ride was fun but Sam and Tommy had gotten soaked with the icy water during the ride and they were shaking like tambourines when they finally finished. Memories of that cold time filled his mind as he turned into a small park along the river to get out and walk awhile to pass the time. He stopped at a picnic table and sat down to watch the scenery and think about Cheryl. The quiet serenity of the park, for he was the only one there, soon got to him and he started to doze off, but he roused himself after awhile and got back in his old Ford and drove some more miles to pass the time.

It finally became time for him to pick up Cheryl. He followed the directions that she had given him and was soon at her house, but he didn't stop at the third house from the corner he stopped at the second house from the corner. He didn't want her to see his old beat up car until they were walking to it, afraid she would slam the front door on him if she saw it before then. He opened the car door and as he started walking up to the front door he began getting that old nervous, shy, feeling again.

When he got to the front door he knew that there was no backing out then, so he rang the doorbell. In a few seconds Cheryl was there greeting him in a friendly manner which allowed him to relax a bit. She led him down a hallway to see her brother and sister-in-law. Sam grew a little anxious again even though he had already met them and thought they were nice enough people, they were still strangers and he still had to impress them, and deceive them. Deceiving was something that he had gotten much better at since he had started making his little weekend trips to the "Greenwood", but this was the first time that he had taken it so far. Although Sam thought that they were good people he was willing to do almost anything that was not illegal to get to know Cheryl, so he would deceive them. He walked out of the hallway, with Cheryl, into the living room that was carpeted with a thick white carpet and finished with a white leather sofa and love seat, and not much else. The left side of the room had a large picture window that looked out on a patio and a small yard surrounded by flowering bushes and other plants. Sitting on the sofa, with two boys who looked to Sam to be around ten years old, was Danny watching a large television with the boys. Nancy was just coming into the room when Cheryl said, "Sam you remember my brother and sister-in law."

"Sure it's good to see you both again." Then Cheryl said, "These two little monsters are my nephews Bobby and Jimmy." She then smiled a mischievous smile and said, "Or should I say Robert and James." Sam could tell that they did not like to be called by those names as they looked with mock anger at Cheryl who simply turned away from them smiling to look at Sam and say. I'll get my purse and be right back and then we can go." Sam while watching her leave said, "Okay." Then Danny jumped off the sofa and grabbed Sam's hand to shake it vigorously and almost yelling said. "Hello Sam how are you doing?" Sam a little startled by his sudden outburst stepped back and said. "I'm doing good. How about you?" Looking Sam up and down he said. "Sam you're a pretty big guy did you play football in high school?" Sam had never thought of himself as big being around five feet ten inches tall and weighing a hundred and eighty pounds. Sam was glad he asked that question though because he loved football. "Yeah I played in high school. I played tackle on both offense and defense my senior year, and we had a great year my senior year we only lost one game and tied for the district title.

"That's great! How did you do in the playoffs?"

"We didn't get to go. The team we tied with for first in district got to go. We came close but we had to stay home."

"That's to bad Sam."

"Yeah, but it was a big thing for a little town like Crescent that does not have winning teams in any sport very often, and they have not had a winning football team since. The year after we left they lost every game."

"You should have tried college ball."

"I did play when I went to Southern Oregon College." Sounding surprised Danny said, "You went to college?"

"Yes, I went for two years and played on the freshman sophomore team they had for a few years there. I never did make varsity. I was invited back to play on the varsity for my third year but that was when I left the school. Danny sounding more impressed by Sam said, "You must have been pretty good to have played in college, are you going to go back and finish College?" Sam uneasiness had long left as he answered. "I would like to someday. I need to save some money though and that's has been hard for me to do, but I'm going to get serious about saving one of these days and go back to school." Cheryl walked back into the room carrying her purse and in a scolding tone of voice said, "What are you trying to do give Sam the third degree," He's afraid I'm going to turn out to be an old maid." Her brother stood saying nothing and looking uncomfortable, but Sam could tell that Cheryl was only acting out, as she continued. "Sam let me rescue you from my brother. We can go now if you want." Sam was still thinking that he was going to like this outspoken girl with the rough edges and sense of humor. As Cheryl stood there waiting for him he saw that she was wearing the same denim coat and carrying her big black purse from the night before. Sam said his good-byes and started walking down the hallway with Cheryl leading the way down the narrow hallway. Sam opened the door so they could leave and as she did Nancy yelled. "Cheryl do you have a key to the house?"

"Yes, your little girl will not wake you when she comes in tonight." Then turning to Sam as they walked towards his car she said, "They treat me like I'm a teenage girl who's going to go out and get in trouble." She did not say it hatefully and Sam could tell that she had a great deal of affection for her brother and his family, and they also seemed to have equal affection for her, and he felt like he was getting a feel for her outspoken but caring style. As they walked Sam started worrying about her seeing his beat up old car and how it would affect her, but more importantly, as they neared the car he needed to think of something to say to her and he was having a hard time doing that. So after they entered the car there was an awkward silence. Sam was always tense around a girl like her, a girl he hardly knew yet a girl he was so very interested in. She was not close enough to touch him, but she was very close, and he was very aware of that, and it was not helping his thinking. He knew he had to say something quickly though, or she would think him a nerd so he said. ""I'm sorry about this beat up old car but its all I have right now. I had a nice Pick-Up but it broke down."

It's alright Sam. I've always liked older cars. I bet it will get us where we are going."

"It runs alright. It won't break down on us."

"That's all that's important Sam." Sam liked what she had said. The more that he was getting to know her the more he was getting to like her, but he didn't believe for a moment that she really like old cars especially one's like his. As the tension eased for Sam a little he said. "I know it is a little early to be picking you up to go to the Drive-Inn, but I thought we might drive around Springfield and Eugene and get to know each other before it got dark." In a friendly tone she said. "Okay Sam that is fine with me." Sam then turned the ignition key to his car and drove off down the street. Cheryl spoke almost as soon as they began moving. To Sam's relief since he was having such a hard time coming up with anything to say. "What is the name of the movie we are going to see tonight Sam? Danny takes the Eugene Register Guard newspaper and I looked through the whole paper but could not find it."

"Yeah, they should have had it in the paper. I have used it plenty of times to find movies. Your paper must have been missing the section with the movies in it." She had caught Sam in a lie because he had no idea what movie was playing let alone whether it was suppose to be good or bad. Thinking quickly though he said, "I've forgotten the name of the movie but I heard that it was a good one. A couple of friends have seen it."

"Do you know what it's about?"

"No, I don't. My friends just told me that it was a good movie and I needed to see it. I think I will drive down Gateway to Eugene that will take up some time. Is there anywhere you want to go?"

"No Sam I don't care where we go."

"I'll drive to Eugene then. Have you ever been to the River Center Mall?" It is like that big mall in Portland. That giant inside mall. The mall with the skating rink in the middle of it.

"Yes I have been to the River Center. Nancy and I go there because it is one of Nancy's favorite places to go shopping. We have spent a lot of time shopping there since I've been here. I think it is Nancy's favorite place's because it is one of the few places that she knows how to find. We go there almost every day." Sam then said, "They haven't lived in Springfield that long then?"

"They have only been here for four months. The reason they invited me down here is because they know so few people here, and since Danny is gone so much Nancy has gotten lonely and wanted some company, but I have really enjoyed it down here." About that time they passed the Mall, and Sam said as they did, although he thought it was dumb. "Do you want to walk around the mall for awhile? I'm low on cash until next Friday, when I get paid, but we could look around the place until it gets dark."

No, Sam I really don't want to go to the mall. Nancy and I were over there this morning.

So I have seen enough of it for one day." Trying to think of something else to do to pass time. Sam thought he had just enough money to take Cheryl to a fast food joint. That is if he didn't buy anything to eat or drink at the Drive-Inn so he said, "I don't have a lot of money, but I could get you a hamburger at Macdonald's."

"I'm not really hungry Sam but it was nice of you to offer." So they continued to drive and talk, with Sam talking more than usual finding it so very easy to talk to Cheryl. As she looked around the city as they drove she said, "I like it down here. It is so quiet and the traffic is so much better."

"The traffic is terrible if you ask me."

"It's not compared to Portland. You don't know how bad it can get until you have driven in Portland. It takes my brother-in-law almost an hour to get home because of the heavy traffic at quitting time." Sam looked surprised as he said, "An hour that is a long time to be stuck in traffic maybe I don't want to live in Portland."

"No Sam I don't think you want to live there."

"I think that it would be a great place for an exciting weekend."

"Maybe, but I have lived there so long I don't see Portland as exciting."

"Okay Cheryl I am not going to move to Portland. I'll just stay in my exciting little town of Crescent." Cheryl then looked over at him thoughtfully and said, "Sam what is it like to live in Crescent."

"It's a little town of around four thousand people. It has a big lumber mill just outside the city where a lot of the people work, and two dams within five miles of the city limits. I think having those dams so close is one of the best things about living there. We swim at the dams a lot, and sometimes go water skiing, and the hills surrounding the town and dams are covered with Douglas fir trees."

"It sounds like it would be a nice place to live."

"I guess it's alright. I have just lived there so long I would like a change. Have you ever heard of the Bohemia Mining Days Celebration?"

"I think I saw something about it on television a couple of weeks ago."

"It is a big thing in Crescent, and about the only thing people outside of Crescent know about the town." Sam was feeling so at ease sitting there talking with Cheryl as they drove on through Eugene. He felt she was trying to get him to like her, just as he was trying to get her to like him, and he was not feeling any pressure to impress her. He was just being himself and that seemed to be enough for her. As they passed the city limits sign and started out into the country Sam had no trouble keeping the conversation going as he said, "Do you really like the "Greenwood?"

"It's great, I like it and really enjoyed myself last night."

"You must like country music then?"

"Yes, I like country music not as much as my brother does, but I like it. I really like all kinds of music." Sam didn't think that Cheryl would like country music. He continued to think that she was kind of hippie and the image he had of hippies was that of a bunch of college aged kids in old work cloths singing folk songs about peace accompanied by flutes and guitars. He didn't think she was a full fledged hippie though just that she might believe in some of their ideas, and Sam even liked some of their ideas. Peace and love was a nice dream, but to Sam it was not the real world. She was intriguing him and the more he got to know her the more she intrigued him. As Sam drove on through Eugene on his way to Springfield he said. "It is starting to get dark so the Drive-Inn gates should be open. We can drive over there now, and we should not have to wait too long for the first feature to start. So Sam drove his old Ford through Springfield and out to where The Cascade was located. It was still light out when they arrived, but the gate was open so Sam drove on in and paid the Cashier. There were only two cars parked in the Drive-Inn when they drove in so Sam could park anywhere. He drove towards the back and parked. Then he rolled his window part of the way down, and hung the speaker on it, and doing that reminded him of something that happened while he was in college. He thought it would be a good story to tell Cheryl and it would give him something to say so he broke the silence." While I was in college I drove off without taking the speaker off the window, and I tore the thing off the stand."

"That happened to a friend of mine while we were in high school."

"Did he put the speaker back on the stand, or turn it in?"

"Of course he did."

"Well my roommate kept the thing and made a speaker out of it for his record player. He regretted it later. He had a fake ID he wanted to use to buy beer since we were underage. It was a card that we guys get when we register for the draft. He changed his birth date on it to show he was twenty one so one night the two of us tried it out at a little store. When he went in to try it, the clerk told him he was running a check out on his cash register, but if we came back in a half hour he would sell him the beer. We should have known there was something fishy about that, but we were young and dumb. When we pulled back into the store parking lot a police car pulled in right behind us with its lights flashing. I was scared because the card that he changed had written on the back of it that if any one made changes to the card they could spend six months in jail and pay a ten thousand dollar fine. The police accused of us of trying to use the fake ID and then they searched my friend and right away found the fake ID card. The cop turned the card over right away and read the part about the jail time and the fine. Then he said we were in trouble with the federal government, and that was very serious, and I was in as much trouble as my friend. I was really scared and just knew that I was going to end up in jail. My friend, Roger was his name, had left his billfold back in our dormitory and the cops wanted to see his drivers license so they had us drive back to the dormitory and when we got there they followed us up to our third story room. They found the Drive-Inn speaker Roger had hanging on the wall and that is when they really got mad and I knew by then that I was absolutely going to jail. They told me that even though the speaker was hanging over his bed, and he admitted taking it, and he had the fake ID. I was still in as much trouble as he was. I didn't think that was right especially when Roger had to talk me into going in the first place, but what could I say. They then had us drive down to the police station. When we got there they took Roger into question him and left me alone to worry and sweat, but when they had finished talking to him, they said to my great relief that I could go but Roger had to stay. They had called his parents and they were coming down to pick him up driving three hours on the highway to do it. I drove his car to the dormitory feeling very lucky. I don't know what went on when his parents got there or if he was charged with anything. He would never tell me and I never asked. That was one scary night that I will never forget. I also know that I will never forget to put a speaker back on its cradle again before I leave a drive-inn." Sam was feeling more and more at ease with Cheryl finding it easier and easier to talk to her as the evening went on and on, which was not always the case when he had been out with other girls. Cheryl had sat so quietly beside him watching him and listening to his story. He had from the very first time he talked to her, and got his first real good look at her, out there on the dance floor of the Greenwood, thought that she was intelligent and that was one of her attractions for him. Thinking that he turned to her to say "Cheryl did you ever go to college?" She didn't answer at first as she stared ahead with Sam continuing to watch her, but she eventually turned her head slowly to him and said. "I was planning on going, but I got married pretty young and that ended those plans." Sam surprised said, "You were married! Then trying to be funny even though he was married he turned to her smiling and said, "You're not still married are you?"

"No! I've been divorced for four years now. My husband did not want to work. I ended up supporting him until I got tired of it. He was a musician who played in a band that did not play very much and he did not want to get a regular job."

"Did you have any children?"

"No thank god we didn't."

"Yeah you are right about that."

"It really wasn't much of a marriage and I try not to think about it. It was not a happy time in my life. He was not much of a man and he used drugs and was abusive. I put up with him for a year, but we were apart much of that time. I took all I could take. Now I've just tried to remove him form my memory." Sam found himself feeling sorry for her as he watched her sitting so still staring ahead speaking, in a low tone of voice, with her face expressionless. By that time the afternoon had turned into night so Sam and Cheryl's attention turned to the screen to watch the flickering images. They sat there in the darkened car, not speaking, with each of them trying to watch the movie. Sam had absolutely no interest in the movie with Cheryl sitting so close to him. It did not help that it was a terrible movie. To Sam it was like a weird fantasy making absolutely no sense to him. He was not trying very had to understand it though. He remembered that he had told Cheryl that it was suppose to be a good movie so he said, "The guys who told me this was a good movie sure didn't know what they were talking about. This is a terrible movie." Cheryl quickly said, "Yes it is." Then as they sat there in silence again with Cheryl sitting so close to Sam and him so very aware of it he built up enough courage to put his arm around her. Then the car got so very quiet. So quiet that Sam could not only feel her breathing as the arm that he held around her rose and fell to the rhythm of her breathing, but he could hear her breathing. Sam's senses were on edge as he felt the softness of Cheryl beneath his arm. He was excited yet so scared that she would move away from him. He felt Cheryl also get excited as the rhythm of her breathing increased. He did not want to say a word afraid to break the spell they were in. To Sam there was no movie on the screen, no car surrounding them, no floor beneath their feet there was only Cheryl. If he had to have spoken at that moment he could not have put two words together to speak. Sam waited as long as he could before he started to lightly squeeze her towards him. He then turned towards her as she turned her face to meet his and they joined together in a passionate kiss and Sam's spirit's soared. Sam then pulled her tightly to him squeezing her body against his showing the frustration that had welled up in him. The sensations of Cheryl and the joy he felt in her allowed him to kiss her, and with such passion, were lifting him so high he could have flown. He was feeling as good as he had ever felt in his life and the feeling lasted as long as the kiss lasted and it lasted as long as Sam could hold it. Cheryl eventually pulled back not abruptly, like she didn't like the kiss, but easily. She continued to lie lightly in his arms as they watched the screen with both of them breathing much faster now. While there was tenseness in the car before, as they both worried about impressing one another, now there was only joy as they both knew this would not be their last date. They both now felt they had found someone who really liked them, and someone they wanted to like them. From the moment that Sam left Crescent that day there was not thought of his wife or his child there was only his new obsession with Cheryl. While he sat there feeling so comfortable, with his arm snuggly around Cheryl and wondering if he should say something, Cheryl broke the silence; "Sam would you get me a coke? I'm getting thirsty." Happily he said, "Sure I will! I am getting kind of thirsty myself." With that he jumped out of the car and headed for the concession stand almost running because he was feeling so good. He was definitely only living in the moment and oh what a wonderful moment it was. Sam brought two cokes and was soon back to the car opening the door to smile at Cheryl and say, "Has the movie gotten any better?"

"No, I think that it has gotten worse if that's possible."

"Well maybe the next movie will be better."

"I hope so." When they had finished their cokes Sam again put his arm around her and to his pleasure she leaned against him. He had been a little worried because she had so abruptly sent him away for the drinks. When it came to women Sam was never sure of himself. Though when she gently leaned against him his worried vanished and his confidence returned. He soon turned to her and she turned to him and they kissed and continued to kiss long intense kisses with Sam eventually laying Cheryl back on the seat, and there they stayed enjoying the sensations of each other until the lights on the screen flicked off. They then slowly sat up blinking their eyes as they adjusted to the bright lights that shined into the car. Sam made sure the speaker was put back on its cradle and then started his car to drive it slowly out of its parking place with Cheryl sitting cozily beside him. He then followed the long line of cars that led out of the Drive-Inn. They didn't talk much as Sam drove Cheryl home with his arm around her. They were both sleepy and tired especially Sam who was usually asleep much earlier than when they left the Drive-Inn that night. He was feeling so close to Cheryl as he held her, and was sure she was feeling the same way, and they did not have to say a word. They had been strangers uncomfortable with each other just a few hours earlier now they were so close that Sam felt that he could almost tell her that he loved her and mean it.

He had never felt this way about any of the girls he had picked up before at the Greenwood. The few girls that he was able to coax to leave with him he never saw again and never wanted to. He had never wanted them to get so close that it would be hurtful for them to stop seeing each other. Sam's idea when he started his drive to Springfield that night was that he and Cheryl would just have some good times for a little while leaving some good memories for both of them. Cheryl would never have to know he was married. He was finding out though that he was already having feelings for her. He now knew that his relationship with Cheryl was going to be much different than what he thought it would be, and he wanted to and definitely would date her again. Sam was soon driving up to Cheryl's brother's house where he walked Cheryl up to the front door to kiss her and tell her he would call her soon. Then he turned and left very happy and very sleepy to drive home to Crescent and his family.

Chapter Three
The Mohawk

The next day at work Sam could not keep his mind off Cheryl. It is dangerous working in the woods if you don't keep your mind on your work, but it was a very hard thing for him to do that day. From the time that he rolled out of bed that morning she held his thoughts. Thoughts that made him feel good and made his work day pass very quickly but a little dangerously with his mind not completely on the job. He knew he was going to see her just as soon as he could, and that was the first day he could afford it, the day he got paid, Friday.

That evening, sitting at dinner, with his wife and son, he was thinking about Cheryl, and after dinner watching television he was thinking about Cheryl. Brenda could tell he was distracted because he was not as talkative as usual. He would often feel her eyes on him that evening, but he did not acknowledge her, content with his thoughts of Cheryl. Later on that evening he started feeling guilty so he played with his son and tried to give his wife and son the attention that he always gave them. By Thursday, though, he had called Cheryl and made a date for the next day. He still had a little apprehension when he made the call but his time he was very sure that she liked him. Friday, Sam made his excuses and was off to see her. He had decided that he would take her to a tavern in Springfield. It was a place he had driven by many times and always wanted to check out. The Mohawk looked much larger than the neighborhood taverns that he had been to. It was a long, single story building, painted red with one of its long windowless sides facing the street. It had a gravel parking lot in the front and back, and above the entrance was a large luminous sign with an Indian head painted on it, and big black letters that spelled Mohawk Tavern. After he and Cheryl entered the tavern, Sam could see why the building was so big. The place was filled with pool tables; far more pool tables than Sam had ever seen in a tavern before. The room looked like a sea of green felt. There were a few tables and booths here and there otherwise that was it except for the pool tables. Sam ordered a beer for him and Cheryl and the two of them settled down in a booth. Looking around the large room he said to Cheryl. "

"This place looks more like a giant pool hall than a tavern. Cheryl looking around the room said; "There are a lot of pool tables in here. It reminds me of a few places in Portland."

"I've never seen a place like this. I guess I don't get around enough coming from little Crescent. Do you have a favorite place in Portland where you do your drinking?"

"I have some friends, who like to go out and drink, and sometimes I go with them, but they don't stick to one place. My brother Jim has a bar he goes to almost every night." Looking surprised Sam said, "Every night!"

"Yes, I think he is an alcoholic. He always wants me to go drink with him and his friends. I go sometimes. He pays for my drinks."

"Well that's a good deal there."

"He lives in a house boat."

"He lives in a house boat?"

"It's his home. It's kind of a neat place, but very small. It's like a floating mobile home."

"That's something that I've never heard of, someone actually living full time on a house boat. My brother-in-law has a little houseboat but he just uses it to go fishing. It's way too small for someone to live in.

"My brother's boat has plenty of room for him."

"Does it have a separate bedroom?"

"Yes, it has a bedroom, a small kitchen and a living room. He has been living in it for a long time and really likes it. Of course all he does is work and drink now. He was married at one time and has two children who live with his former wife." Sam could not get over the idea that someone lived in a houseboat thinking it was such a great thing to do as he said, "They have places in Portland, then, where people can permanently dock houseboats?"

"Yes, they have lots of people who live in house boats in Portland."

"It sounds great but I don't think I could live in one. I get seasick. I went fishing in the ocean near Reedsport and I got sicker than a dog. I don't know if you have ever gone deep-sea fishing, but I can tell you when you go over the bar it can be very rough."

"My brother's boat hardly moves. It's hard to even tell that you're on the water. What's the bar that you crossed?"

"At Reedsport and other ports it is where you first enter the Ocean coming out of the dock area. They tell me that it is always rough right there. I know it was when I crossed it. I felt ashamed about getting sick because my father was in the Merchant Marines during the war. I was the only one who caught a fish though. I caught a sole. It's a funny looking fish very flat and round with both its eyes on the top side. It's a bottom fish, so if I hadn't let too much line out I never would have caught it; in fact I think I snagged it when I was pulling the line in. I really did not know what I was doing because it was the first time I had ever been deep sea fishing and I was very sick. They say that a sole is a real delicacy, though, and a very expensive dish at restaurants."

"Did it taste good?"

"I don't know. In fact I don't know who finally got that fish." After they had a few more beers with Sam beginning to feel its effects he looked at Cheryl and said; "Do you play pool?"

"Yes, but I'm not very good. The bar that my brother goes to has a lot of pool tables and they are always playing pool so I play with them."

"Well I'm not very good either so it should be a good game. Sam was actually thinking that he was going to win easily, since she was a girl, and she had seemed kind of clumsy, though in an endearing way, at the Greenwood. He did think that she had danced great, though, with a smooth coordination, but he really thought he was a pretty good pool player. It had been years since he had played, though, but he was confident as they started the game. When she won the first game he thought that she had been lucky so he definitely wanted to play another game so he could show he was the better pool player. After she won three games in row he was ready to quit. His pride was bruised and he was feeling angry that he had let her beat him. He knew he was feeling chauvinistic, and it was not like him, but he would not, or could not feel any different. He sure was not going to let her know how he felt, but it was not easy for him to let on that it did not mean a thing to him. All the way back to their booth, that was on the other end of the long room, he kept fighting to keep a friendly expression on his face, careful not to let her see his game face. Though it was hard by the time they got back to the booth he had the painful loses behind him. He sure did not want to mess up the wonderful relationship he was developing with Cheryl. When he sat down he was concentrating only on how much he enjoyed being there with her and how much he liked her. They then settled down into their booth and started some serious drinking. That night Cheryl kept up with Sam beer for beer, even after Sam started getting that slightly drunk, but not yet drunk feeling, that he loved so much. When he looked across the table at her he knew that that she had to be in the same daze he was in, with her eye lids partly closed, and with a slight smile, and an unfocused look on her face. Later that night, as they were sitting quietly drinking Sam looked up to see Cheryl staring at him before she said, "Sam how many brothers and sisters do you have?"

"I come from a big family. My parents had six children. I have three sisters and two brothers and they are all grown and living there in Crescent. That is why I want to leave. No, seriously, I love my brothers and sisters and am glad they live close."

"Are you the oldest child?"

"No, I'm one of the babies of the family. The three oldest are much older than the three youngest. The oldest kids were mostly grown and gone while my younger brother and sister and I were growing up. So what about you how many brothers and sisters do you have? I know you have two brothers."

"I also have a sister. There was just the four of us. My sister is married and lives in Portland." As the night wore on they got to know each other much better talking easily and comfortably. They were both talking but Cheryl more than Sam. During the night Sam began to feel that Cheryl really liked to talk, but that did not bother him, in fact he liked it because it was helping his conversation. Although usually a quiet guy, he was finding he wanted to talk to her and it was easy for him. His wife was not a big talker. He felt that was one of their problems they seldom had conversations like he and Cheryl were having that night at the Mohawk.

After spending more than three hours getting to know each other they left the Mohawk. Sam had spent much more than he had expected, and ended up with only two dollars left in his pocket. He had no idea that Cheryl would drink as much as she had, but she had matched him beer for beer the whole night. He had never known a girl who could drink as much as she did that night. Feeling half drunk, and very content with Cheryl squeezed up next to him, he pulled out of the parking lot and headed for her brothers house. After parking his car in front of the house, they kissed a long and lingering kiss and Sam was settling in for many more of the same there, in his car. While Sam was holding Cheryl so very close to him, though, she said something that got him very excited. Turning and looking directly at him she said softly, "Sandy and the boys went with Danny to Klamath Falls today. They're going with him this time so they can have a little family vacation. Since no one is home do you want to come in for awhile? We will have the house to ourselves." Sam was absolutely delighted and very surprised. He had expected them to make out for awhile, and then he would walk her to the door and leave. So Sam answered quickly, "Yes! I would love to. She then led him into the house, he not believing his luck. She went to the television and turned it on then threw some cushions from the sofa on the floor. "I like to sit on the floor." Sam liking the night more and more said, "So do I." Leaning against the pillows, they started watching a movie. Sam lay there full of anticipation as Cheryl said; "Do you want something to drink?"

"No, I'm not really thirsty." Drinking anything was the last thing on his mind right then.

"I think I will get a coke. I'll be back in a minute." Sam watched her leave. When she got back she put her drink on a coffee table. Sam wanted to hold her so badly but not wanting to seem too anxious waited. He could not and did not wait very long though before he put his arm around her, she snuggled up against him and they started kissing. After awhile he laid her down on her back, with him on top with his lips never leaving hers. As he lay over her he pulled her tightly to him feeling the softness of her entire body underneath him. He then reached around her to start unfastening her bra and to put his hand up under her white blouse to fondle her large oh so soft breasts. She pulled away from him breaking the spell, "Lets go lay in the bed it is much more comfortable. Sam was groggy from coming out of his trance, that Cheryl had broken, and his lack of sleep, but he certainly understood what Cheryl was offering so he said, "Yes, it would be." She then led him into the bedroom where she sat on the edge of the bed, and started taking her cloths off. Cheryl was soon undressed and lying underneath a sheet waiting for Sam. He had watched her as she undressed, with pleasure in his eyes, while he took his cloths off, and was looking at her as she smiled up at him from the bed. He returned her smile and then slowly pulled the sheet back to slide in beside her. He put his arms around her to pull her tightly to him. Kissing her long and lingering kisses before rolling over on top of her and thinking how much better she felt with her cloths off. Her skin so smooth, cool, and sensuous, he moved his hands slowly down the sides of her body to her legs. His hands rose slowly to her stomach and then to her breasts to linger long in their ample softness, before moving to gently caress her face. As they rolled on the bed Sam noticed a very loud squeaking sound coming from the bed springs. At first it did not bother him, but the noise seemed to grow louder and louder. Soon the screeching started affecting Sam becoming so irritating to him that it was like the feeling he got when someone was scraping their fingernails on a blackboard. The sound was so loud and distracting that Sam, who would have enjoyed the fore play much longer soon, gave into the noise, and completed the love making. Sam's face contorted into a look of ecstasy, and with the sound of the screeching seeming to fill the entire house and finally reaching a crescendo as Sam felt a intense pleasure that approached pain. Then they fell on their backs breathing heavily completely drained of energy. Sam was feeling so good laying there enjoying the pleasure with his chest rising and falling, but so glad the screeching had ended. Sam lay there smiling; then the thought that Cheryl might expect him to stay all night entered his mind. He knew he had to get home to his wife she would not understand him staying out all night. So getting nervous knowing that he had to get going home soon, he told Cheryl that he had to go to work in the morning. Seeing that she looked disappointed, he made sure he gave her a passionate kiss knowing that she had expected him to stay. Then they quietly walked slowly through the dark house to the doorway and when they got to the door, Sam said, "I'll call you when I get off work tomorrow." He then kissed her again and left to go to his home. Driving home very tired and sleepy he was feeling so good his mind filled with thoughts of that night and making love to Cheryl. As he drove on in the darkened car he began struggling with some tough thoughts though. He began to think about his wife and his child and that he might have lost them if he had stayed out all night. He felt guilty about his growing feelings for Cheryl and the time he was spending with her. He was feeling so bad, about how he might have lost his family if he had stayed out all night, that he decided right there and then to never see Cheryl again and run as far and fast as he could away from her. He would not let her ruin his marriage. On his very infrequent one night stands, after he got what he wanted he was gone and never looked back. He had never wanted to date any of them or even see them again. He was afraid of his feelings for Cheryl, though, so he would never see her again. He even promised himself that he would spend the rest of the weekend with his family and never even visit the Greenwood again. He thought it might hurt Cheryl for awhile if he never saw her again, but his family was what was important. So with those thoughts secure in his mind he quit worrying and drove home. The next morning Sam woke a little later than usual after the long night, but he felt great and Brenda had a nice breakfast waiting for him like she always had for him on the weekends. She had Scrambled eggs, sausage links, and pancakes with maple syrup his favorite breakfast. He didn't like to eat breakfast real early in the morning, like at five thirty in the morning, the time he woke up during the week to go to work. He did like a nice big breakfast when he woke up later in the morning, like he did on most weekends. It was a nice sunny fall day so he took his little family to the City Park and played with Patrick. Playing catch with him with a small rubber football and pushing him on the swing. Then at noon they ate a delicious picnic lunch of fried chicken and potato salad. Sam and his little family were very happy that morning with Sam's only thoughts on them. He was right back into the comfort of his family life. Everything seemed so right with him being the husband and father that he was raised to be. He had no conscious thoughts of Cheryl. It was like she never existed as he ran and played with his little boy, and ate the picnic lunch with him and his wife. After the park, they visited Sam's mother and step-father. While sitting there at his folk's house Sam started weakening a little. Thoughts of Cheryl, and of wanting her, started filling his mind and he soon knew he would see her again. He knew it was wrong, and he knew he was weak, but he also knew he would see her. Brenda knew something was wrong, as they drove quietly home, with Sam sitting still and staring ahead lost in his thoughts. She looked at him and said; what's the matter Sam?"

"Nothing, I'm just thinking."

"Thinking about what? You were kind of quiet at your mother's house`."

"I've just been kinda quiet lately. It's something at work. There is someone at work I don't get along with and it just bothers me sometimes. I know I should not let it bother me. I should just punch him in the nose." There was an overbearing guy that worked with him, but he had set him straight right after he started working for Patton and he never had bothered him since. Sam thought it was a good story though and Brenda believed him as she said; "What does he do that makes you mad?"

"The guy thinks he can boss me around and he is not a boss. It is really starting to make me mad."

"Don't you get fired? You know you need that job."

"I'm not going to do anything stupid. It just gets to me sometimes." "Just leave him alone. Don't pay any attention to him."

"That's kind of hard to do when you're in the woods out in the middle of nowhere with just a six man crew. I know I have to get along with him, and I will. It's just that sometimes I think how much I would like to punch him in the nose."

"Sam!"

"Don't worry. Everything will be all right. I'll stop thinking about punching him out, right now and think about you and Patrick. Okay?"

"Okay Sam. I just don't want you to get in trouble." Sam had once thought that he was the most honest person he knew, but not any more. As soon as they got home Sam told Brenda that he was going for a pack of cigarettes, and while he was at the store he used a pay phone to call Cheryl and make a date for that night. It was if he had never made the conviction to not see her again and live only for his family. He never even thought of them after he left the house. There was only the excitement of knowing that he was going to see Cheryl again.

Chapter Four
Hendrick's Park

Eugene is a mid size city that lies almost exactly in the middle of the state of Oregon, at the southern end of the wide and long, and very flat Willamette valley. Although it is not very large city, by most standards, it is the second largest city in Oregon. It's not a mill town like Springfield, it's very close neighbor; it's more of a large college town, greatly influenced by its most prized possession the University of Oregon. At the southern end of this college town, a hill juts out of the end of the valley right next to the famed University. A hill with houses hanging on the steep, brushy, Douglas fir covered side facing the University. On its flat top there are no houses, only a tree covered park and that is where Sam wanted to take Cheryl. He had been out with her quite a few times by then, and they were getting along just great, but he wasn't sure how she'd take just going to a park for a date, because he had always taken her somewhere even if only to play pool at the Mohawk since he had learned how to beat her now and then. He would have liked to have taken her dancing or to the movies or at least to play pool, but he was broke, like he often was now, so he had no choice if he wanted to see her, and that he definitely wanted to do. After he picked her up, and while driving down Gateway Boulevard towards Eugene, he said to her a little nervously. Cheryl I'm pretty broke right now because I've got a lot of bills to pay this paycheck. She turned to look at him and he could see that she had a look of concern which made him feel better as he continued on, "I know where there is a nice little park in Eugene. It's called Hendricks Park. It's up on a hill and it has lots of trees and flowers for you to see. It is really nice. It is full of Rhododendron plants and they are blossoming right now. They grow wild in the woods, and where we are logging now there are lots of them, and they all have flowers on them even up there. They also have fenced in some deer where they have lots of room; it is like seeing the deer in the wild." Sam was talking quickly trying to get everything he had to say about the park said before she had a chance to say yes or no. Then pleading before he finished; "Cheryl I would really like to take you someplace else but I can't. Will you mind going to the Park with me at least this once?" When he had finished she turned to him with the look of concern still there and said, "Okay Sam we can go to the park. You don't have to take anywhere if you don't have the money. We can go for awhile. It's not out in the middle of the woods is it? Out in the middle of nowhere?"

"No! It's right in the city. Every time you go to Eugene and don't take Gateway you pass right by it. It's on that big hill on your left side when you first drive into Eugene. We don't have to go to the park we can drive around Eugene and Springfield for awhile I've got plenty of gas."

"Let's go to the park. I want to see it now." Sam's mood lifted then and they were soon driving up the steep back side of the park, the wild side that did not have the houses hanging on its side. It was covered with brush and small trees that crowded in on the narrow road. Sam drove slowly up the hill, as it was growing dark, trying to keep on the far outer edge of the narrow road, especially on the corners in case there was a car coming down the hill. He didn't want to tell her of the accidents that happened on that road. Cheryl, looking at the jungle of greenery crowding the road, said; "Are you sure there's a park on this hill?"

"Yeah, it's flat on top. We will be there in just a minute. Up there they have a big parking lot, rest rooms, lots of lights, and all those rhododendrons." Just then they rounded a corner and drove onto the top of the hill. A hill that was covered with beautiful, huge, old growth Douglas fir tree soaring into the sky. Brushy rhododendrons and Azaleas and other plants were everywhere. All of them covered with large flowers of various colors and shapes. Sam stopped the car in the parking lot and they got out and looked around, Cheryl said as she took in the scenery, "This is really nice Sam."

"I told you. You didn't believe me did you?"

"I was beginning to wonder coming up here through that jungle, but this is nice."

"I've got a blanket in the trunk we could go lie down in that grassy area over there."

"Yes, it is a nice night to lie on a blanket and look at the stars." Sam got the blanket out and they walked over to a large grassy spot where Sam spread out the blanket. After trying to find the deer without any luck as the evening darkened they lay down on the blanket.

There they lay quietly staring at the very bright stars shining through the towering fir trees. It was so comfortable for Sam laying there that he thought it would very easy for him to go to sleep. With his hand behind his head for a pillow Sam said to Cheryl as he stared, in awe, into the sky. "Look at all the stars out tonight. See the big dipper up there?"

"Yes, I think so." Then pointing to the sky Cheryl said. "Yes I think so. Its right over there isn't it?"

"Yeah, that's it." Continuing to stare at the sky through the limbs of the tall trees, she said, "It's so peaceful looking at he stars."

"They look so big and bright tonight." They quietly continued to look at the stars for a while then Sam put his arm around her while pulling her to him and they kissed. There had been no one in the park when they arrived and Sam had seen no one drive in since then. So thinking no one was around to see them he rolled over so his upper body was on top of Cheryl's breast's, and as he was looking down at her he kissed her passionately. She quickly responded by pulling away from him and saying angrily. "Stop that! What are you doing?" Sam looking as guilty as a puppy being scolded, said, "I was just trying to kiss you Cheryl. That's all."

"We are out in the open. People can see us."

"I don't think there is anyone here. The parking lot is empty."

"I want to go back to the car." Sam was getting a little angry himself. He didn't care if anyone saw him kiss Cheryl even if they were lying on the ground, and that was all he was trying to do. If she wanted to go back to the car though there was nothing for him to do but pick up the blanket and start back to the car. So that is what he did. Cheryl walked back towards the car without saying a word with him worried since he had never seen her angry before. A thought had entered his mind while she was angry. The thought turned to words as they walked, and softly just slipped out without him really thinking about what he was saying. "You look beautiful when you're angry." As soon as he said those words he wanted to swallow them thinking that it was such a dumb thing to say. He just knew he had gotten them from some movie. Luck was on his side, though, because Cheryl said, "What did you say Sam? Sam did not answer her, but flashed a big cheesy, guilty smile on his face, and he couldn't keep himself from laughing at what he had said. Cheryl looked at him suspiciously, "What did you say Sam?" Then stopping and looking at him more closely she said, "What's so funny Sam? What did you say?" Sam looking at her with a smile he could not suppress said, "I didn't say a thing."

"Sam what did you say? Tell me?"

"It was really stupid. I can't tell you." She then took hold of Sam's arm and pulled on it making Sam laugh and pleading. "What did you say? Sam, tell me what you said I won't let you go until you tell me."

"I can't its stupid." It's something I got from an old movie. I had to have gotten it from some old movie. It's stupid really." Cheryl continued to hold Sam's arm and he continued to laugh and pull away as she said. "Just tell me I promise I won't laugh at you." Sam knew he was going to have to tell her there was no getting out of it so he said, "Okay, I said that you look beautiful when you're angry." She looked at him a little puzzled for a second and then said dismissively, "You're right, I've heard that in a movie and it does sound silly."

"I can't believe I said it." By then they had reached the car. Sam worried about Cheryl's mood, but she scooted over next to him when she got in the car and said "There is too much light here with all these lights, here in the park, why you don't drive down that road where it is darker." Sam knew then that she had forgiven him, and was elated. He drove along the top of the hill out of the park and into the darkness under the tall trees. He didn't drive far before he turned off the paved road and onto a gravel road. He parked the old Ford and he and Cheryl stayed the rest of the night talking and making love and this time he told that he loved her. They had been making love almost every time he took her out, and he had been treating her like he loved her for quite awhile.

He knew it was because he did love her so he told he loved her. He still didn't know what he was going to do about being married and still loving his wife though.

Chapter Five
Lum Lees

Things went along pretty good for Sam. He was seeing Cheryl almost every weekend and sometimes during the week. Although his wife made it clear that she did not like seeing him gone so much, she complained little. He was having a great time and didn't want to think about what the future held for him and Cheryl and what he was doing to his wife, or how the world he was living could not last. Those thoughts did not make him feel good and he was feeling so very good about his life. He was going to enjoy this new life he was leading, and so much of it now centered on Cheryl. It was just as exciting as it had been for him in college, and when he had first met his wife.

One Saturday when Sam was not able to see Cheryl he called her just to hear her voice. When he called her voice sounded excited as she said; "Sam, my best friend, Katy, has come down from Portland to visit, and she is going to stay for at least a week. We've been having a ball, and she is anxious to meet you."

"That's great Cheryl. She can go out with us next weekend. I can take the two of you to the Greenwood."

"Danny is taking us tonight. It's too bad that you can't come with us."

"Yeah, it is too bad but I just don't have the money this weekend."

"Katy is really looking forward to seeing you."

"Next weekend is payday so I will be there for sure and with money to spare. Have you been showing Katy around Eugene and Springfield? I know you had to have shown her, you and Nancy's favorite place, the River Center Mall."

"She just got here Sam, but we're getting ready to go there right now. You made a good guess, but you know it is not my favorite place."

"I knew it. I knew you would be taking her there."

"You know me pretty well don't you, or more like you know Nancy. Nancy's waiting for me right now.

"She is anxious to get to that mall isn't she?"

"Yes she is. Malls are her life. She is waiting for us in the car right now, so I have to go. Can you call me tomorrow?"

"Yes, and you know I will call you tomorrow." Sam ended the call disappointed that he hadn't been able to talk to her longer. He was already feeling a little jealous of Katy after hearing the excitement in Cheryl's voice and knowing that she would be able to see her all week long and he wouldn't. Hearing the happiness in her voice did make him happy, though. She seldom seemed really happy to him, and he hardly ever saw her smile. He thought there was a sadness and loneliness to Cheryl, and he could not figure it out. She covered it up with her brashness and wonderful sense of humor, and just being so cool and unaffected, but he still could see it. She was just so funny and entertaining, and she always got him to smile or laugh, that he didn't think about it much. When he did think about it, though, he thought some of her loneliness had to be because she was living in Springfield, forcing her to be away from all her friends and most of her family, and also because she was divorced and single. To him, though, there was just a melancholy that seemed to be part of her. Because of that he was very glad that Cheryl was feeling so good about her friend visiting her. She sounded to him to be as happy as she was when she was playing loudly, with her two nephews.

The next Friday evening came quickly for Sam, and before he knew it he was driving to Springfield to pick up Cheryl and Katy. As he drove up to the house he was thinking that it was good that he had gotten paid that day. He knew, for sure, that Cheryl would want to show her friend a good time and he had now had the money to do it They were looking out of the little kitchen window watching for him so Cheryl and Katy were out the front door and running half to his car before he had even got out of it. Sam watched them hurrying to him like a couple of school girls. Katy he thought was a very nice looking girl. She was thin and athletic and a little over five feet tall, with long curly light brown hair. A smiling Cheryl met him with a big embrace, and as they stood there in each others arms she said looking at Katy. "Sam this is my best friend Katy." Smiling himself Sam said, "Hi, Katy how are you?"

"Hi Sam," I'm doing fine. I finally get to meet you. I've heard so much about you from Cheryl."

"I hope that it's been good things that she has been telling you about me." Cheryl broke in and said then, "Sam you know I would never say anything good about you. Faking a hurt tone in his voice Sam responded, "I knew you didn't like me, but I will be nice and take you out anyway, but since you haven't been nice, you'll have to ride in this old car instead of my red hot corvette."

"Oh, this is a beautiful old car Sam." Cheryl said laughing as they all got into the old Ford. Sam had been worrying again and his worries were bothering him when they entered the car. Sam was what he considered, and he knew everyone thought him to be, a rather quiet guy. He was a little worried about that and other things about himself. He always thought of Cheryl as a smart, big city girl and him a rather slow small town boy. Although he knew Cheryl had not come from a wealthy family, he felt as far as class and intelligence went she was higher in the middle class, than he was, maybe even near upper class level. One on one though they got along great. He knew she really liked him and they were so comfortable with each other. Now there was Katy, and Sam was wondering if she would like a quiet, and a little shy, small town boy who sometimes was low on confidence. If she didn't, would that affect how Cheryl felt about him? It was obvious that Cheryl was very attached to her. So there he was worrying about how he was going to get along with Katy. Cheryl scooted over next to him, and Katy moved in behind her sitting next to the passenger door. As soon as they were on their way Cheryl turned to him and said sweetly, Sam, Katy wants to go dancing. Do you think you would like to take a couple of hot babes out dancing tonight?" That snapped him out of his worrying as he answered Cheryl confidently.

"Well I got paid today so I can afford to show you two hot babes a good time. Sure lets go dancing." Cheryl then burst in saying. "We feel good Sam and are ready to party."

"I guess we can go to the Greenwood. You like country music Katy?" Cheryl answered him, "Sam, she likes country music like I do, but she doesn't like the Greenwood. Danny took us dancing there last week, and she didn't like it." Sam sarcastically smiling said, "She didn't like the Greenwood my favorite place and where I met you?"

"No Sam, she didn't like it, she wants to go someplace close to the University of Oregon in Eugene." That is when Katy jumping into the conversation and said, "Sam I've heard that the guys are crazy there and like to party. I've wanted to come down here for a long time, for years. Everyone has told me how great it is down here." Sam was getting the impression that Katy was not the kind to settle for a working class guy like him and the guys who filled the Greenwood. He thought she must be after some future doctor or lawyer from the University of Oregon, and now after getting a good close look at her he thought that she was pretty enough to attract one as he answered her, "I don't know any places that have live music and dancing in Eugene. I always go to the Greenwood." Katy leaned forward in her seat and looked at Sam and said, "Sam could we just drive through the campus" Then Cheryl broke in. "Yes, Sam could we drive through the campus? I've never seen the campus either. Then maybe we could drive around and find some place.

"Okay, I can take you through the campus if that is what you want to do. It's a nice place with lots of ivy covered buildings and big lawns and big trees everywhere. It really looks like a college campus."

"Sam." Cheryl said, "Katy is only going to look at the guys. She won't notice any ivy covered buildings."

"Cheryl don't tell Sam that." Katy quickly put it. "Don't try to hide it, Said Cheryl quickly, "he will find out about you soon enough." Then Sam almost yelling said. "Hey! I do know a place in Eugene. It's been a long time since I've been there, and I've only been there a couple of times. I don't know if you will like it because there haven't been many people there the times I've been there. It's a Chinese Restaurant Called Lum Lees. It has band and a small dance floor in its basement. The place is really dark with just bean bags to sit on except for a few booths.

The band is small but it is loud," Katy could not help herself as she interrupted Sam. "Were there any cute guys there?"

"I don't know how cute they were, but there were always some guys standing around waiting to ask girls to dance." Katy broke in again, "That's sounds like the place for me. Can we go Sam?"

"Sure, I don't know if you'll like it, but we can go."

"If there are any guys there I will like it." First Sam drove them to the University campus. Sam's dream had always been to play football for the University of Oregon. He had been a fan of the Oregon Ducks since he was in grade school. In the little town of Crescent, all of the boys were fans of the Ducks, or the Oregon State University Beavers. Sam was a Duck and had been on the campus many times while in high school most of the time just to visit the Student Union and to drive around and gawk at the girls with his friends. He also attended sporting events there. Football and Basketball, and to see their famous track team compete at Hayward Field.

Sam and the girls drove on through the campus slowly, driving by the Student Union where they could see students sitting out on the large patio talking, eating, and studying around the small round tables. They drove on, by students crowded on sidewalks with towering trees full of green leaves arching their big braches high over their heads. As they drove, Katy broke the silence saying, "Look at the hunk, Cheryl! He's such a babe, and look over here, there's another one." Cheryl was twisting her head to Katy's directions as they drove by the infamous Pit. The nick-name given to the University's basketball court. The Basketball court that is known around the country because of its loud and rabid fans. Sam had been to many of the games there and always sat in the metal bleachers that hung from the side of the building, something that makes the building very unique. Sometimes when the games got exciting he and the rest of the people in those old bleachers would start stomping their feet shaking the bleachers while looking almost straight down at the players. Sometimes Sam had seen fear in the eyes of opposing players as they looked up at the crazy students shaking the bleachers, staring over the edge, wild eyed, and yelling as loudly as they could yell. Oh how he loved it.

By the time they had finished driving around the big campus, and Katy had enough of ogling the guys, it was dark, time for them to go to

Lum Lee's. Sam drove over to the restaurant and into its back parking lot. As he slowed the car down Katy jumped out of the car excitedly before it was fully stopped, and headed around the building getting far ahead of Sam and Cheryl. She slowed down as she approached the front door so that they could catch up, and when they did she said, "Hurry up! There are guys waiting inside to dance with me." Cheryl scolded back at her, "If you don't stop it, Sam and I will take you to the Greenwood where you'll be able to dance with all those neat guys you danced with last week."

"Okay, I'll be nice." Katy laughed. Sam pushed on the large, heavy, red door, which opened to a darkened entryway. Facing them was a wall that came up about half way to the ceiling and it was topped by a wooden lattice that stretched to the ceiling. On the lattice were two large golden, oriental, decorative plates hanging side by side. Through the lattice they could see a long, mostly empty bar, and to their left there was a large room filled with empty tables covered with dark red tablecloths. Sam steered the girls to the right to a door that opened to a small landing and a descending staircase. At the top of the stairs, standing behind a table with a money box in front of him, was a tall very serous and grim looking oriental man who took Sam's money. As they descended the stairway, they could hear music coming from below which grew louder and louder as they approached the bottom. At the bottom they turned to the left and entered a darkened room whose walls were painted black. Standing there in the entryway they viewed a band blaring music from what looked like a cave carved out of the dirt on the side of the basement on their left. They stood there for awhile adjusting their eyes to the dark room, and then walked ahead past a large concrete wall that blocked their view of the band and the little dance floor. As they came around the end of wall they viewed a large room with a sunken floor in the middle, filled with people sitting on bean bags. There were also a few benches and booths on the ledge that stretched around the sunken floor. At the far end of the room from where they stood was the cave where the band continued to play its music with a few people dancing on the small dance floor in front of them. There were about eight people dancing with a few more than that sitting, or standing around the room. Sam walked towards the back of the room away from the band, where there were a few booths, and the girls followed. Almost as soon as they sat down in one of the booths someone asked Katy to dance. After Sam and Cheryl had sat down and started listening to the music Sam said to Cheryl, "It didn't take Katy long to get asked to dance."

"It never takes her long."

"Well I hope she's having fun. I don't like this music that much. It's too loud and it doesn't have a good beat to dance to."

"We don't have to dance Sam; we can just sit here and drink if you want."

"Wait until they play a slow one then we'll dance." They then sat back and watched the dancers and listened to the music and drank lots of beer. Eventually the band played a slow song. How Sam loved the slow songs when he could hold Cheryl so close. As the night wore on Sam and Cheryl even danced some of the fast dances, and Sam found the music was not as hard to dance to as he thought. The times they were seated they didn't talk much. The place was so small and the music so loud that they had to shout at each other to be heard. As Sam sat there, not able to talk, he thought of how comfortable he and Cheryl had become with each other. How they didn't even have to talk to enjoy each other's company, and how it was almost like they had been married for years. Cheryl would leave to talk to Katy once in awhile. Katy had not come back to sit with them since the very first dance. Later in the evening though she would come back for a few minutes at a time otherwise it was just Sam and Cheryl quietly sitting side by side. When it approached one o'clock Sam said loudly so Cheryl could hear over the music, "I think we'll have to leave pretty soon. I have to work tomorrow and I need to get some sleep." This time Sam was not lying he did have to work. "I have to be up and leave at five this morning. I am going to need some sleep."

"You have to work in the morning? You didn't tell me."

"I know, I forgot about it until now. The boss wants to finish logging the unit we're on and then we'll be ready to rig up, at the new unit, and start logging Monday morning when we first get to work." Disappointed, Cheryl said, "Okay, I'll go tell Katy." Then she left but was soon walking back with Katy. They sat down next to Sam with Katy close on one side and Cheryl very close on the other causing Sam to think something was going on, and he quickly found out what it was as Cheryl put her arm around him and pleaded sweetly, "Sam, Katy found this guy that she really likes, and she wants to get to know him better. Could we stay around a little longer?" Then Katy, pulling on Sam's left arm said, "Sam, I will love you forever if you just stay a little longer. I really like this guy. Please, Sam." He was really tired but being the nice guy that he was, and always wanting to please Cheryl, he said, "Okay."

"Oh thank you Sam!" Katy yelled, "I won't forget this, "Then she hugged Sam tightly and scampered off to see her friend. Sam knew then that he did not have to worry about Katy liking him. He settled back into his seat feeling tired enough to go to sleep even with the loud music blaring in his ear. He had been working a lot of overtime and it had worn him out. He leaned against Cheryl and tilted his head onto her shoulder. She asked him if he wanted to lay his head on her lap. After he did he was soon asleep. A little later Cheryl shook him awake and told him she had to talk to Katy and then left him leaning forward with his head down and half asleep. She was gone for a few minutes before coming back to sit beside him again, "Sam, I have something that will help you stay awake. It will give you energy and make you feel a lot better." Only half awake he said. "What?"

"Sam I can give you one of my diet pills. These pills will give you energy. They'll keep you awake you won't feel sleepy anymore, and you can take one in the morning to keep you alert at work tomorrow. Sam, trying to wake up completely said, "I don't think that I want to take any pills." As sleepy as Sam was he didn't think there was a pill in the world that could keep him awake that night, especially a diet pill. Cheryl was insistent as she said, "Sam I've taken these pills many times and stayed up all night, and I was never sleepy in the morning."

"Cheryl, a pill is not going to keep me awake." Cheryl gave up trying to convince him and left to talk to Katy. When she got back she eased up close to Sam and whispered, "The pills I want you to take are amphetamines. Have you ever heard of them? Some people call them whites or white crosses. Truck drivers use them to stay awake when they drive at night." Sam had heard of truck drivers taking pills called bennies to stay awake, but he knew they were illegal and addictive, so he said. "Are these pills legal?" Cheryl looking at Sam now and speaking with passion said, "Sam, these pills are the same thing as the diet pills I've been taking to lose weight for the last six months. My doctor gave me the prescription to get them. They are legal. If I had a diet pill I would give you one, but I don't. These pills are the same thing they won't hurt you but they will help you stay awake. These whites should be just as legal as my diet pills, because they are the same thing." She took a plastic sandwich bag filled with small white pills out of her pocket, opened it and handed him one. Sam looked at the little white pill with a cross etched in it dividing it into four equal parts and said, "Cheryl if it's not legal I don't think I want to take one." Sam knew the law got very serious about people who used drugs and could not believe Cheryl was using them, he didn't think she was that kind of person, and although she did not think they should be illegal they were and they could be arrest for having them. Sam had experimented with marijuana a couple of times out of curiosity, but he had just got very hungry and felt nothing else. He had not liked the people who smoked it, and the fact that he might get arrested using them, and did not want to have anything to do with the people or their drugs after the few times he tried marijuana. As he sat there though with Cheryl looking at him so earnestly, he changed his mind about taking the pills. He loved Cheryl and she didn't seem to think she was doing anything that was really wrong in using the pills. So he swallowed the pill feeling that it would not affect him anyway, just like the time he had smoked marijuana. After a short while Cheryl asked him if he felt any different. He told her that he did although he didn't, just like he had expected. Sam ordered another beer though and did not lie down like he had before, but sat up with Cheryl and listened to the music and was able to talk to, or yell at her during songs. Finally Katy came back to the booth and told them that she was going to ride home with the guy that she had met. Cheryl wanted to go have breakfast with them so she could find out more about what the guy was like who was taking her friend home. Sam went along with the idea although he knew he should have gone home to get some sleep. They ate quickly though and then Sam drove Cheryl home to Springfield. He was fully awake, but Cheryl fell asleep on his shoulder. Sam was thinking that maybe the pill might be working since he was so wide awake. Far from being sleepy; he found he was very sexually aroused, and wondered if it was the pill that was doing it. He couldn't help himself as late as it was and as tired as he had been, he wanted to have sex with Cheryl. She though obviously just wanted to go home and go to bed, but Sam very much wanted to have sex so he drove past her house. It was a small neighborhood that was more a part of the country than the city. There were lots of open fields around and secluded places where Sam could go to park. So Sam drove slowly trying to find a place. He soon came to a bean field. The vines for the beans were strung on wires between posts that were about five feet high. They looked like grape vines but had clumps of long green beans dangling from the vines. Sam drove into the bean field to a small clump of trees at the end of the field. Cheryl was still asleep and didn't want to wake up. Sam was so wide-awake and wanting sex as bad as he ever had in his life and wondering even more if the little white pill he had taken had anything to do with it. He knew he would not be able to have sex in the car. So on the ground Sam started kissing her and she kissed him back for awhile until she fell asleep again. Sam woke her up and this time she was very receptive, but she soon cried out in pain as he tried to lay on her. Sam looking for the first time at the ground could see that they were lying on rocks. Sam sat up very frustrated and stared at the street lights in the distance upset knowing this night he would have no sex no matter how badly he wanted it. To his astonishment, as he sat there staring, he could see the sky was lightening up as the sun was just about to come up over the horizon. He wondered where the time had gone. He just could not believe that it was morning already, and he knew that he had missed the crummy because they always picked him up long before the sun came up. He was feeling scared as he drove Cheryl home. He helped her walk to the door making sure she was awake and could walk into the house. Then he kissed her before leaving her to drive home. He knew because he had missed his ride to work he might have lost his job. He was feeling like an idiot for seeing Cheryl and putting his job in jeopardy. He knew that he couldn't afford to lose the well paying job he had with Boney. He could only hope they would give him another chance. He promised himself that he would never take a chance like this again to put his family in jeopardy. Again he promised himself that he would never see Cheryl again. The fear about losing his job held him all the way home and did not leave him until he got home and got into bed to fall asleep beside his wife. He would worry about it when he woke up.

CHAPTER SIX
LOGGING

When Sam got up that morning, Brenda told him that she had gotten up when the Crummy honked for him, and had told his boss that he was not home. She said that he didn't seem to be mad. It made Sam feel much better. Then he told her why he had been out all night. He was no longer so worried about staying out all night because Brenda had let him get away with so much. So he told her he had been out drinking with friends at a tavern, and when it closed they had gone to one of their houses to drink and play poker. She let it go at that, like she had been doing, making Sam feel that she believed him.

Sam still was apprehensive Monday morning. He really didn't feel like he had been working for Boney long enough that his job was real secure. He was even worried that the Crummy might not even show up. He woke up an hour early that morning and quickly dressed. Then lying back in his recliner he waited with his thick wool socks on his feet. He never put his cork boots on until he got to the logging site because of their spikes. He was relieved when he saw the lights of the Crummy shine on the large picture window in the front room. He jumped up opened the door, and walked quickly to the Crummy and got in. He sat down in the third and last row of seats in the Crummy, which he always had to himself. He felt very relieved when the boss, or the hook or hook tender as he is called in the woods, said nothing to him about missing work. He felt very lucky and promised himself it would never happen again. He would never put his job in jeopardy again. Being that it was five in the morning and still dark out, Sam lay down in the seat and went to sleep like he did every morning. He always slept soundly in the back of that old dust filled truck, with the only sound coming from the whine of the tires as they rolled down the highway and that sound never bothered his sleep one bit. It was a long two hour ride up into the mountains above the Mackenzie River. First they drove to Springfield and then along the river to the dinky little town of Blue River, then up into the mountains on a winding gravel road for another half hour. The loud sound, of the tires on the gravel would always wake him, but Sam would continue to try to sleep as best he could as the Crummy wound its way up the mountain, going higher and higher up into the high Cascade Mountains.

When they were almost to the work site, Sam would sit up and put his cork boots on. Then He'd be ready to work that morning, with the hook tender, Palmer, and the other choker setter, Stud. His big leather cork boots reached half way up his calves offering him some protection from the brush. Covering the bottom of the boots were short metal spikes that would bite into the thick bark or the slick skin of a log, if the bark had been scraped off, keeping Sam from slipping and falling when running or walking on the logs.

There had been five men in the Crummy on the trip up into the woods. There was Palmer, the hook tender, Sam and Stud the choker setters, Jim the Shovel Operator, and Mike the Yarder Engineer. The Landing Chaser Pete drove up in his own little pick-up from Blue River where he lived, and Boney drove up in the company pick up. Sam knew these men's faces very well, having worked with them for over six months. He started working for Patton Logging Company early that summer when he was over weight and out of shape, and very happy to get the job. He had been out of work for over a month when he was finally hired by Boney. He and his little family had been living on the money he made from a part time job, while he had been out of work, so he was very glad to get the job. It was late June and the temperatures were in the nineties when he first went to work. He had gotten an old pair of rotting old cork boots that his stepfather had sitting on his back porch for years, and on his first day of work caught the Crummy at a downtown service station, carrying his cork boots, and a lunch pail that was painted red, and wearing a tin hat, all of which he had borrowed from his retired stepfather. That first day of work was very hard on him. They were working on the side of a steep hill that had absolutely no shade, and Sam after working most of the day out in the hot sun, walked forty yards out of his way to lay his head under a small tree. The tree was about half the size of a Christmas tree and pulled out of the ground and pushed sideways with most of its needles gone after a log had been pulled over it. Sam didn't care that it provided practically no shade; it was the only shade he had been under all day. Palmer and Stud got a good laugh seeing him lying under that sorry little tree. He soon was used to the hard work and heat though, and even started enjoying the job.

Sam got out of the Crummy, on that cold winter day, and stepped onto the landing, an area on the top or near the top of a hill that is cleared and leveled by a caterpillar tractor. It has to be large enough to hold the Loader and the Yarder. The loader is the large machine that loads the logs onto the logging trucks. It swivels around and clamps onto logs with its big metal teeth, looking like some primitive dinosaur chomping on it prey, and then it drops the logs onto a logging truck and its trailer. Sitting beside it on the landing is the Yarder another big machine. It is the machine that pulls the logs into the landing. The Yarder sits on a long metal flat bed trailer, like the ones pulled behind the big Semi's, on the highways, though it is much longer. In the middle of the trailer is a very large winch with a big spool of thick cable spooled around it. Sitting up beside the spool is a square metal cage with glass covered windows where the Yarder engineer sits and runs the machine. The thick cable from the spool runs up a tall metal pole standing at the end of the trailer. The pole looks like a wider metal telephone pole. After the cable runs up the spar pole it runs through a large pulley at the top and then down to the very bottom of the hill to run through two more pulleys, or blocks as they are called in the woods, and then back up to the Yarder. Two, short, thinner, cables that are about twenty feet long, hang close together from one of the lines that run down the hill. The two cables are called chokers and they're used to hook the logs that lay down the hill from the landing. Palmer, Sam and Stud are the ones who wrap the chokers around the logs, and hook them so the logs can be pulled into the landing to be loaded onto the trucks and sent down the mountain to the saw mill.

Sam walked to the edge of the landing and then down the steep hill into the brush to where they had finished up logging the day before. There Sam and Stud waited for the Yarder to start up. Palmer was up the hill looking to see how they were going to pull the last few logs that remained on the unit out. As Sam stood there he heard the Yarder start, and looking up the hill the saw a plume of black smoke spew from its smokestack, just like it did every morning. He knew it would not be long before the big machine picked up the heavy cable, the main line lying on the ground in front of him. The main line was one of the two cables, the biggest one, that Sam, standing there, could see run up the steep hill to the Yarder, and the one that the short chokers hung from. The chokers hung about four feet apart from the main line at the Butt Rigging, the very heavy metal connectors. The Chokers being much thinner and lighter than the big Main line cable, made it possible for Sam to pull them though the bush to the logs. As he stood in the cool morning air he heard three loud horn blasts from the top of the hill. The sounds were coming from the big horn hooked to the Yarder. The main line with the rigging, lying in front of them, jiggled a little then lifted slowly into the air lifting the tangled chokers off the ground. Palmer, now with them, had squeezed the rubber handle ,that hung from a belt at his waist, three times sending electrical signals to the Yarder which had caused the horn to blow three times, and that was the signal for the Yarder Engineer to lift the main line. Palmer squeezed the rubber handle again and they heard another honk and then the Main Line stopped rising, leaving the chokers hanging about half way of the ground. Sam grabbed the end of one of the chokers and started dragging it to a log that Palmer had picked out. It was a big log that came up to his waist and it was lying flat on the ground. Sam threw the end of the choker over the log and then climbed on to it. The spikes on his cork boots dug into the thick bark helping him climb and then held him steady once he was on top. Sam was now in great shape, better, he thought, than when he played football. He jumped off on the other side of the log and grabbed the stiff choker about four feet from the end with his gloved hands. Sometimes there were breaks in the outer wires of the choker, which was made from many small wires wound together, and those broken ends, sticking out from the wire, could rip a bare hand. On the end of the choker was a nubbin, a metal plug about three inches long and a little wider around than the choker. Sam grabbed the stiff choker tightly and started jamming the nubbin end under the log. The ground was soft but he could not get the choker all the way under the log so he got down on his knees, and started scrapping out a hole under the log. Then he tried to jam the choker through again and this time the nubbin broke through to the other side. He quickly jumped back over the log grabbing the nubbin at the end of the choker and locking it into bell making a clinking sound when he did. The bell was a small square piece of metal a little bigger than a person's hand. The choker ran through a hole in the top of it so it was able to run the full length of the choker. The bottom of the bell that hung from the choker was hollowed out so that you could stick the nubbin in and lock it in tight. When the nubbin was locked into the bell, the choker worked like a cowboys lasso. Sam would set the choker on the log or lasso it so it could be pulled into the landing by the Yarder. After Sam locked the nubbin into the bell with a clink, he ran far enough away to be safe. Stud, who had finished setting his choker, was waiting for him with Palmer. Palmer signaled the Yarder Engineer, with a single toot, to start pulling the logs into the landing. Sam turned to Palmer after the logs had moved up the hill, and they were safe said. "How many more turns do we have left."

"It looks like we've only got about six more turns to go. Boney wants us to finish up this unit and unrig the Yarder. He also still wants us to move it to the new site today, but leave it to be rigged up tomorrow."

"How far is the new site?"

"It's close. It's just up this road about five miles; it will be easy to log." The logs are big and the ground's not steep. It's on a flat spot on top of this mountain." We could log it with a Cat, but Weyerhaeuser won't let us, they think a Cat would dig up the ground to much." Sam smiling said, "It's about time we got something easy." They seem to give us the steepest ground and the hardest logs to get every time. I think we get the units that no one else wants." Stud then threw his two cents in. "Yeah, don't be to sure about this great unit we haven't started logging it yet."

"Right, you are Stud." Sam said, "I'll have to see this unit to believe it." Palmer smiled, "Believe me, it's a great unit, the best one I ever logged with Boney. Sam, did you listen to the Oregon game last night? They played a great game against UCLA." Yeah! I could not believe they won that game. They were supposed to lose by fifteen points." The clinking of the bells, hanging from the end of the chokers, as they banged into each other while they were being dragged back through the bush interrupted their conversation. Sam heard a honk coming from the landing after Palmer had squeezed the rubber handle and chokers stopped in front of them. The three of them rushed to set the chokers with Stud being the last one to get to them like always. Stud somewhere in his fifties, was almost as tall as Sam but very thin, balding and slightly humpbacked. To Sam he looked weak and fragile. He was also slow and followed Palmer around ready to his bidding in a moment's notice, like he was constantly afraid of losing his job. Something that Sam did not like. To Sam it looked like it would be hard enough for him to walk down the street, yet he was climbing hillsides and setting chokers. Palmer showed little respect for him and was the one Sam believed started calling him Stud in the first place, to make fun of him. Sam had not wanted to call him Stud, when he first started working for Boney, but it wasn't long before he started calling him what everyone else called him. Sam was to gain some respect for the old guy though, because even if he looked like Ickabod Crane, he always kept up, somehow, with seemingly little effort, always getting to his log and having his choker set by the time Sam had his set. Palmer was usually around to help him, though, and if there was an easier log or a closer log, he got it. Sam didn't care because he prided himself in going after the hardest log, and doing it by himself, and most of the time he was able to do it.

Sam thought that Palmer was a good hook tender but he didn't like him very much. He was too arrogant for Sam's liking, and although he knew arrogant, sometimes went with being a boss; he thought Palmer over did it. He did always pick the best and easiest logs to set the chokers on, and helped him and Stud set them. He also did a good job of watching out for their safety, but that was something they all had to do for themselves all of the time. Palmer did his other job to. He moved the big heavy metal blocks when all the logs lying up the hill under the main line that could be reached by the chokers were pulled into the landing. The main line then had to be moved over to where the logs were lying. So the Blocks, or the big metal pulleys that the big lines ran through, had to be moved. The blocks weighed about sixty pounds and consisted of two round heavy metal plates hooked together with a wheel that ran freely between them for the lines to run on, and a hook on one end of the plates so it could be attached to a stump. Palmer would throw the heavy block on his back, when he had to move one, and then slowly walk, with his heavy load over the brushy ground, to where it was to be hooked to a new stump. Sam knew he did his share of the work and did it well, but he thought he had little respect for anyone but himself and would let everyone know in his snide little way. There was not a lot of communication between him and Palmer except for what had to be said to get the job done. Palmer did like the Oregon Duck football and basketball teams which gave Sam something to talk to him about but there was little else.

The logging unit that they were finishing up on was very steep and it had been hard for them to log. Climbing around a steep side hill was tough, so it was a good thing that Sam was now in great shape. He knew he would never been able to log that unit when he first started working for Boney. They were on the last logging road and had to pick up some logs at the very bottom of the hill, but there was a problem. When the tree fallers had gone through the unit to fell the trees and then buck them into logs. They had cut or bucked some trees and snags that the wind had blown down. Since the snags, or dead trees, and the live trees had been blown down their roots had come out of the ground. Where the fallers had cut the fallen trees at the stump they had left a stump and a large tangle of roots that they called a root wad. If the tree had been a big one, the stump and its roots could be larger than a Volkswagen Beetle. The last row of logs that they were logging had a big one perched at the top of the hill close to where the logs were being dragged into the landing. From way below, to Sam and Stud it looked like a big dark hairy ball. Its stump was at least five feet across there it had been cut off, and its huge roots were caked in mud. As two big logs were being dragged up the hill they watched them intently to see if they would disturb the giant root-wad. They knew that if it were knocked off the little stump that was holding it on the hillside; they would have to start running. They had walked sideways across the hillside far enough to be out from under the logs being dragged up the steep hill. It was something they always had to do just in case the chokers broke and the logs came charging down the hill or they knocked something down the hill. They knew that if the root-wad got knocked loose, although they did not think it likely, there was a chance that the bouncing ball could bounce far enough sideways, on the steep hillside, to reach them.

The turn of logs did not knock the root-wad from its perch, but the main line did sway over enough so the logs nudged it a little. That caused Sam to crouch and get ready to run but then relax and stand up when it did not come off its little stump. When the chokers came back and Sam and Stud rushed in to set them, they kept their eyes on the hillside, because after the thing had been nudged, it could come down at its own. When they hurried out after setting their chokers, Palmer was waiting for them. He had been up on the landing talking to Boney. When they approached, he said, "Have you guys been watching that root-wad?" Stud spoke up quickly. "Yes, we saw it Jim. We've been keeping our eyes on it."

"Well, you guys keep watching. There are just two turns left. I'm going to move the extra block over so we can send it into the landing when we're finished. I'll call for the haywire when you send the last turn of logs in."

"Okay, Jim," Stud said, "I'll call for the haywire if you want."

"No, Stud, I'll call for the haywire." Palmer walked off through the brush. When the chokers came back to the landing, Stud squeezed the whistle hanging from his belt. They heard the honk come from the top of the hill and then the main line stopped in front of him, leaving the chokers dangling with their bells clinking in the air. They rushed in to set the chokers on the logs that Sam had picked out. Stud had the extra whistle and was suppose to be the boss, or the rigging slinger, when Palmer was gone, but he would take all day to pick out the logs so Sam started picking out the turns of logs, out of frustration. Stud didn't care and seemed happy to let him do it. It was a good thing because Sam might have quit because of his frustration and Stud knew it. When they had finished setting their chokers, they rushed out and Stud signaled the Yarder, then the logs started slowing climbing up the hill. This time the logs hit a stump just after starting up the hill and it sent them off on a different path than the other logs had taken. They were heading up the hill in a straight line to the root-wad. Sam, with adrenaline rushing through his veins, turned to Stud who was looking wide-eyed up the hill and said. "Dam they're going to hit that root-wad." Stud didn't have to be told as he said, "Look out! Its goanna come!" They could not run until they knew the path it was going to take or they might run right under it. So they stood crouched, ready to run either way, watching the logs intently as the neared the small stump that held the root-wad. The logs hit the stump and stopped. Then the engine on the Yarder roared loudly as it pulled harder, tightening the big mainline until the logs popped over the stump and plowed into the mud caked roots, of the root wad pushing it away from the stump it was on. It rolled over and then hesitated before starting to slowly roll down the hill, picking up speed, going faster, and faster until it was roaring down the hill. Sam, feeling relieved, said, "Good, It's going straight down the hill." Then it slammed into a huge stump, sticking out of the side of the hill, sending mud from it roots flying everywhere, and sending it bounding into the air thirty feet. Coming down it hit an even bigger stump, this one sending it reeling sideways in Sam's direction. Sam said almost inaudibly, "Dam." Then the root-wad started rolling and bouncing here and there like a ball in a pin ball machine, all the time quickly getting closer to Sam as he stood staring at it frozen. He was crouched down and his muscles were tensed ready for him to spring either way just like when he was playing football, but this time his life was on the line. The thing was rolling to his right and was going to miss him, but then it hit something and turned straight for him not more than twenty feet away going a hundred miles an hour. He leaped to his right and while diving he saw a flash of movement out of the corner of his eye as one of the stumps big dangling roots slapped the ground hard with a loud Whap right beside him, missing him by inches. He kept running long after he knew the root-wad had missed him and he was safe. He turned around, breathing heavily, and with his heart racing, to see the root-wad lying quietly and so serenely, at the bottom of the hill, in a small creek with muddy water gushing around it. Stud started walking towards him from about fifty feet away. He had not been close to Sam so the root-wad missed him easily. As Stud neared him, Palmer came up behind Sam and yelled at Stud, "What the hell were you doing Stud! Didn't you see that those logs were going to hit that root-wad?" Stud didn't say a word but just stared at the ground. Palmer very near him glared and then started yelling again. "Dammit! You almost killed Sam! How dumb can you be? Couldn't you see what those logs were going to do? How long have you been working in the woods? Twenty years? Thirty years?" Then Stud said, "I know, Jim, I should have been watching better." That caused Palmer to explode. "Stud, you've got to be the dumbest choker setter that ever worked in the woods. I ought to fire you right now and send you down the road. I'm going to tell Boney what happened and tell him that he should fire you. I'm going back now and get that block that I left back there. After this turn of logs goes in, I'll call for the haywire so that you can send the blocks in. When I get to the landing I'll tell Boney what happened." He turned then in a huff and stalked away. Sam, while Palmer was yelling at Stud, had forgotten about how scared he was, and how he had just narrowly missed being killed. He had felt sorry for Stud as he walked to where he was standing. The two of them stood, not saying a word, staring up the hill waiting for the chokers to come back. Sam did not feel that Stud deserved to be yelled at, and knew that he wouldn't have done anything different than he had done. He had thought there was very little chance that the root-wad would come over as far as it had. So far that it almost hit him. Sam also wondered why, since Palmer, who saw the root-wad, hadn't done something about it. He was the boss, the one with all the experience. He could have put a choker on it and pulled it into the landing. He also knew that there was little chance that Boney would fire Stud. Choker setters were too hard to find. There just weren't many men that liked to do the hard, dangerous, dusty in the summer, muddy in the winter, sweaty work. Sam jerked when he first heard the jangle of the chokers as they were being dragged back from the landing. He was tense and on edge, the effects of having such a close call just minutes earlier, as he hurried with Stud to set chokers on the last two logs in the unit and send them in. Palmer called for the haywire, which is a much smaller cable that they send back in place of the big thick line and is divided into sections that can be unhooked where the sections meet. He stopped the haywire with a squeeze his whistle, the rubber handle hanging from his belt. Sam then unhooked the hay wire. Then they hooked the blocks to it and sent them in, and they were done logging that unit. They climbed up the steep hill in the soft dirt of the big deep furrow that the logs had dug in the ground while being dragged into the landing turn after turn. It was much easier for them to walk there than in the brush. They were walking in line behind the slowly moving blocks as they were being pulled into the landing. As they walked Stud lagged behind Sam and Palmer. When they got to the top of the hill and the landing, it was a busy and noisy place. The big loader's engine was roaring as it was swiveling back and forth picking up the last of the logs and loading them on to a waiting logging truck. The short, stocky landing chaser, holding a small cigar in his teeth, was unhooking the blocks from the haywire and carrying them over to hook to the Yarder. While he toted the heavy blocks on his back, he was carefully watching the Loader, staying out of its way, as it quickly swiveled back and forth and clamping its giant metal teeth to logs. The Yarder Engineer was lowering the guy lines, the cables that were hooked to the top of the Spar Pole. The tall metal pole that the main line ran up before it ran down the hill to the blocks. The tall pole gave the main line its height off the ground enabling it to lift the chokers and making the logging so much easier. The guy lines ran from the top of the Spar Pole in all directions to be hooked to stumps and tightened to keep the pole secure. They kept the Spar Pole from being pulled over when the heavy logs were being pulled into the landing. Sam, with Stud's help, walked around to each guy line and hooked to them from the stumps they were unhooked so they could be winched into the Yarder and their ends hooked to it. While they were pulling slack on one of the guy lines so they could unhook it. Palmer walked over from the landing and said to Stud, "You're lucky, Stud. Boney said that he would give you another chance, but one more mistake like that and he will send you down the road. Stud, Sam could have been killed." Stud answered softly. "I'll never do that again Jim. Tell Boney that."

"You'd better not if you want to keep your job. You and Sam keep unhooking those guy lines so we can get them into the Yarder, We want to get moved out of here soon so we can and get the Yarder moved to the new site, and hooked up and ready to log before dark. "Right Jim," Stud said quickly. They soon had the lines unhooked and then they were pulled in and hooked to the Yarder. Then the Spar Pole was lowered down onto its cradle on the Yarder, and the hydraulic outriggers, the big metal legs with their big round flat feet, were lifted up and pulled in. The outriggers were set down to lift the trailer to keep it steady and to keep pressure off the rubber tires. The big Yarder, which could be driven, was ready then to drive to the new site along with the loader. Palmer drove Sam and Stud on ahead, to the new site where they picked out the stumps for the guy lines to be hooked to. Then, they went around to each stump and with a small chain saw cut notches in them where the guy lines would be wrapped around them to secure the lines on the stump. They finished notching all the stumps, and then took the blocks down into the brush and hooked them on stumps. They were ready to rig the Yarder. It wasn't long before they saw the Yarder and the loader coming slowly up the road. After the Yarder was very slowly and very carefully parked in just the right position so that the guy lines matched up with the notched stumps, with Boney yelling out the directions, and seemingly on the edge of blowing his top, like he often was, the day was done.

That was it for that day as they saved the rest of the rig up until Monday morning. The whole crew except for the landing chaser, Pete who drove down in his little pick up, climbed into the crummy then and headed down the hill with Palmer driving. It was dark as they drove down out of the mountains and everyone was quiet, and very tired, after the long hard day. At the bottom of the mountains they neared the Mackenzie River. The crummy, not so old but very used after many a dusty mile in the mountains, drove off the gravel road and onto the pavement under a giant dark green canopy of tall fir trees. There at the edge of Blue River, Sam called out to Palmer, "If you stop I'll buy the beer." Although Palmer didn't like to stop for beer and he didn't drink, he had reminded them when they first wanted him to start stopping for beer that is was against the law to have an open container of beer in a vehicle, so they could get him and them in serous trouble. He would always stop, though, whenever they wanted him to, which was usually, two or three times a week as they took turns buying the beer. So Palmer turned into the parking lot of a small shopping center in Blue River where there was a small grocery store. Sam jumped out of the crummy and walked to the market in his deer leather slippers. He had long since taken off his big cork boots. It wasn't Sam's turn to buy beer, but he wanted a beer so bad he was going to buy. He pulled eight 16-ounce beers out of the cooler. That would give everyone in the crummy two beers except for Palmer. As tired and thirsty as Sam was, the two tall beers would have him feeling good by the time they got to Crescent. He took the beer to the counter and waited in line. When it was his turn to pay he smiled and said to the clerk. "Don't you think we should get a discount? We buy a lot of beer at this place. The clerk lifted his tired head for a second and looked at Sam and then ignoring him he went back to checking out the next customer, in the long line. Sam just grabbed up his purchase then, and carried the bag full of beer to the crummy. There was something about working hard all day that had Sam always wanting a beer to drink at the end of the day. He thought it was a great reward for him.

The long ride went quickly, the crew drinking beer and talking about the latest news in the Crescent Express, the local weekly newspaper. They were always more talkative when they were drinking beer so before the crew knew it the crummy was driving into the city limits of Crescent over a tall railroad overpass, and then it drove into the parking lot in front of Sam's apartment. There feeling very good he grabbed his lunch pail, cork boots, empty beer cans and climbed out. He walked through the door to his home and family lifting up his little boy up and swinging him around the room saying to his wife. "I'm as hungry as a bear. Is supper ready?"

"Yes, Sam, your supper is ready." He knew it would be ready and he knew it would be delicious like it always was because Brenda was a great cook. That was definitely one of the benefits of being married to her. After he let his boy down he said, "What's for dinner?"

"Meatloaf,"

"Great, I always like your meatloaf just like all of your cooking."

"Sam, you'll eat anything I put in front of you"

"Yes I will, Honey, because you're a great cook."

"Now you say that, but you will probably go out tonight since it's the weekend won't you?"

"I was thinking about going out tonight. Coming home I had a couple of beers with the guys in the crummy, and now they want to go to the Oasis and play pool and drink some more. Tomorrow we can go out to the drive-inn."

"Sam you go out too much."

"I'll stop going out so much, I promise." She didn't answer him knowing he was going to go out no matter what she said. Sam showered and ate, and not long after that he was off down the road feeling very excited about seeing Cheryl after a long day in the woods. He did not worry about his close call anymore because he had many of them while he had been working in the woods. The thoughts he had just recently had about losing his family and his job by seeing Cheryl had completely disappeared.

Chapter Seven
Fatefull News

Sam and Cheryl went to a movie at the Cascade drive-inn one night after they had been going together for quite a while. Driving to the Cascade brought back wonderful memories for Sam, of their first date. He was feeling so very good as he drove to the Cascade anticipating a wonderful night, but for some reason Cheryl was quieter than usual. Sam wondered if there was something wrong as he pulled in beside a speaker and parked. After he hung the speaker on the side window and turned up the volume, he leaned back in his seat. He definitely felt by then that Cheryl had something on her mind. He soon found out what it was as she looked at him with a serious look on her face, "Sam, Nancy took me to the doctor yesterday because I've been getting sick lately." Sam looking at her with a concerned look said, "What was wrong?" Then speaking in a low monotone, without looking at him she said, "Sam he told me that I am pregnant. Nancy thought I was since my period is very late." You could not have hit Sam any harder if you had hit with your fist. Of course, since he had not used protection, he knew that she could get pregnant. Sam had naively felt that the chances were slim since they had sex so seldom. Sam had been so very happy since he had met her, and always looked forward with great anticipation to the weekends when he could see her. His happiness that evening, though, had sunk into a deep hole. He loved Cheryl. Oh, how he loved Cheryl. He had told her many times, yet he still loved his wife, and although he now felt he loved Cheryl more, he was not ready to leave his wife. He had been struggling with the dilemma, but felt he had plenty of time. He had been living in a world that could not last. How his beautifully colored balloon had burst. Oh, how it had burst. Now he had to tell her he was married, and he knew it would break her heart for he knew she loved him dearly. He sat there without saying a word while Cheryl stared at the screen. He knew what she wanted him to say, but he could not say it for he was already married. Feeling so very bad for what was going to say to someone he loved, he turned to her and said sadly, "Cheryl, I would love to marry you and raise our child but I can't, because I'm married." Cheryl turned to him as he stared ahead with his head held low. With the pain of knowing that he had just lost her love forever, and the guilt of knowing what he had done to her, his voice rose with emotion as he continued quickly, "I know that I have been dishonest, and what I have done to you is terrible, but when I told you that I loved you I meant it. I did mean it and I do love you so very much and I will love you forever. I love you more than my wife. I have kept going out with you all this time because I love you. You are such a wonderful person and in no way deserve what I have done to you." Sam was feeling so bad for Cheryl, and himself. She had turned her head away from him and was looking out the passenger window. Sam could not see her crying but knew she was. Looking at her like that his heart ached to hold her and comfort her. Feeling that he did not deserve to hold her, and she would not let him, he did not even try. Soon he could not stop himself, though, and he did put his arm around her. Although he thought she might despise him, and might even throw his arm off, she did not. While sobbing softly, she put her head on his shoulder wetting it with her tears. Feeling so relieved that she did not hate him, he held her tightly as if that would keep her from leaving him. Then with Cheryl held in his arms he said softly, "I love you and cannot stand the thought of being without you. I love my wife, but I love you more. I want to leave my wife and be with you. Then suddenly he lifted his head and wailed loudly crying and saying decisively, with tears in his eyes, "I will leave my wife! I love you too much to lose you! I cannot leave you! I will not leave you!" Then Cheryl lifted her head off his shoulder and said in a calm voice, "Sam do you have any children?"

"Yes, I have a little three year old boy." Sounding very unemotional compared to Sam Cheryl calmly said, "Sam you can't leave your wife and little boy. They need you." Sounding very emotional Sam said, "You need me to. I love you!" Sitting very still Cheryl calmly replied, "I love you too Sam, but you have to think of your family." Sam could not believe what he was hearing. He knew for sure that she loved him and wanted to marry him, but she was thinking of what was best for his family. It made him feel like even more of an ass. He knew the right thing to do was to stay with his wife and child, but the thought of losing Cheryl was making his heart ache. He felt as bad as he had ever felt in his life. He had deceived his wife and had deceived Cheryl and now he was paying for it. Cheryl was out of his arms and sitting quietly beside him when she abruptly but in a low voice said, "Sam I want to go home." The way she said it made him now wonder if she had started to hate him. He knew that he deserved that hate. Worn out emotionally and not knowing what to say, to keep from losing her he just said, "Okay Cheryl," and then he started up his car and drove out of the drive-inn. Feeling so guilty and sad he said nothing as he drove her home. She sat just as quiet, but was still sitting close beside him. When they got there he knew there was nothing he could say to ease her pain and he didn't deserve to say anything to her. When she opened the door to leave, Sam didn't get out to walk her to the door like always, feeling that she wouldn't want him to. He just told her that he would call her knowing full well that she might not talk to him.

He drove off to Crescent feeling miserable, knowing the enormity of the pain and suffering that his deception was causing Cheryl, and would cause her in the future, and how much it hurt to lose her. Sam wasn't ready to leave his wife, but after what happened that night he knew that he might. He loved Cheryl so much that he just could not stand the thought of not seeing her again. He woke early the next morning with thoughts of Cheryl and the night before filling his worried mind. The dilemma that he had been struggling with, but with no sense of urgency to solve was now very urgent. Though he could not tolerate the thought of losing Cheryl he still could not stand the thought of losing his wife and child. Cheryl had told him to stay with his family, but she was pregnant and needed him, and he knew he needed to keep seeing her. There were times, though, that day when he thought he would take the coward's way out and never see or call Cheryl again. Why not, he thought a coward is what he was, along with being an ass. The thought, of never seeing her again, never lasted long because his feelings for her were just too strong, and he felt such a responsibility for what he had done. So that evening he made his excuses to his wife, but this time she got madder than usual. He was starting to feel that she would not allow him so much freedom in the future, but he got his way and drove to the nearest public phone. While he was dialing he hoped Cheryl would answer. He didn't want her sister-in-law to answer for she would now know he was married, and he felt lucky that her husband was on a long sales trip. Cheryl did answer the phone, to Sam's relief, and said softly, "Hello." Sadly also Sam answered, "Hello, Cheryl, It's Sam." Then suddenly worried that she would say she would never see him again he said quickly, "I'd like to see you tonight if I could?" She answered in a voice full of melancholy, "Okay, Sam. I'm not doing anything you can come over." Very relieved Sam answered. I'm in Crescent right now so I'll be there about seven."

"Okay, Sam."

"Great, see you soon."

"Bye." He had worried that she would not see him, but now he knew he would see her at least one more time, and oh how bad he wanted to see her. Driving up to Springfield he was thinking that he didn't know what he was going to say to her because he still did not know what he was going to do about his life. Although he needed to stay with his wife and child he did not know what he would decide. It was his same old dilemma. He knew he had been living in a selfish fantasy world that had to come to an end. He arrived at the house and walked up to the door still not knowing what he would say to her. To his relief it was Cheryl who answered the door bell. He felt very lucky then that her brother was out of town because he knew he would not have let him see her. When Cheryl opened the door, Sam's heart soared, but she did not say a word, and just walked past him to his car not looking at him staring straight ahead. Following behind her he could not help feeling good that see was willing to see him. She got in the passenger side, but did not scoot over to sit beside him like she had always done before. So Sam drove away slowly with Cheryl staring ahead in Silence, and him feeling that this might be a very brief and sad night for him, and the last time that he might ever see her again. How he yearned to put his arm around her and comfort her, but he knew he had no right to do that, and she would not let him anyway,   He was feeling sad enough to cry when the most wonderful thing happened. Something that he did not expect, and felt he in no way deserved. Cheryl scooted over next to him and while leaning on him put her face on his shoulder. Sam's spirits lifted as he put his arm around her and squeezed her close to him like he had done so many times before, but this time he felt the wetness of her tears on his shoulder causing his eyes to well up in tears also. The dark cloud that hung over his head with the thought of leaving her had lifted. The sun was again shining brightly over his head. Cheryl still loved him, so his world had not been destroyed. Then Cheryl said just over a whisper, "Sam, where are we going tonight?"

"I thought we could go to Hendricks's park unless you want to go somewhere else?"

"No, I don't want to go anywhere else. Hendricks's park is where I wanted to go." Sam had wanted them to be alone so they could talk and share their pain and was glad Cheryl seemed to want the same thing. So they held each other while driving through the dark night to their spot in the park. The quiet serenity of the car, and it was serene and even happy because they were both glad to still be together and in love, was broken when Cheryl lifted her head from Sam's shoulder and said with pain in her voice, "Sam, why did you do it?" On edge emotionally tears started flowing out of Sam's eyes, clouding his vision as he drove through the dark night. He cried out loudly, "I don't know!" And again he wailed, this time even louder, "I don't know! It was such a terrible thing to do and I hate myself for it! There is no excuse for what I did and I will never be able to make it up to you! I do love you so much Cheryl and I will love you forever!" Sam was holding Cheryl tightly to him. It was as if he thought that if he held her tight enough he would not lose her. As the car drove up the hill to Hendricks's park. Sam slowed way down on the corners because he was driving with tears welling up in his eyes causing the road to blur in front of him making it a very dangerous ride. Blinking steadily to help his vision he made it safely to the top with tears still in his eyes. Sam was so very emotional knowing how close he came to losing Cheryl and how he still might. Neither of them said another word until they had driven along the top of the hill to their secluded gravel parking place. There Sam still feeling terrible blurted out quickly, his voice pitched high with emotion and determination, "I'm going to leave my wife! I mean it; I'm going to leave my wife! I'm going to tell her tonight just as soon as I get home. You and I are going to get married and raise our child together. Cheryl sitting quietly beside Sam and sounding much calmer than him said, "Sam I can't let you do that. You already have a child you have to think of." Cheryl's calm demeanor helped Sam to cool down as he answered her, "I know Cheryl but I love you, and I need you, and I want to be with you forever, and you're going to have my child."

"But, Sam, you're married to your wife not me."

"I can change that. I can be married to you. I can get a divorce."

"You have to be reasonable Sam. You can't just leave your wife and child for me."

"I can and I will."

"Sam, you're not going to leave your wife. I know that you still love her and you can't and shouldn't leave your son."

"Yes, I still care for her and I love my son, but I love you so very much. Even if I leave her I will still be a father to my son, and would see him often." Sam knew that was not true because his wife's family lived in another state. If he left her she would certainly move back in with them, and he would seldom be able to see his son. At that moment, though, he did not care about anything but his love for Cheryl, and the thought of losing her was driving him crazy. Pulling her close to him he said, "I can't live without you, Cheryl." She came to him willingly wanting him as much as he wanted her. He kissed her a very passionate kiss, while holding her so very tightly, that lasted, and lasted, and lasted. Then he laid her back in the seat and they made love with more want, need and intense passion than they had ever made love before in their lives. The though of losing each other fueling the fire that engulfed them. They then fell back into the seat exhausted and quiet but feeling so good. There they sat at the edge of the park, side by side, looking out at the park darkened by the very huge and very tall Douglas fir trees that surrounded them. Trees that kept the light of the full moon from shining down on the sad lovers. As Sam sat there with his arm around Cheryl, holding her close to him, and looking out into the dark night he now knew for sure she was not going to leave him. He was not going to lose his tough, funny, yet sensitive girl. They sat there long after they had made love with Sam holding Cheryl comfortably and neither of them talking. Both of them knowing how close they had come to losing each others love. They did not talk about Cheryl being pregnant or about Sam leaving his wife that was something that they would put off for another night. Eventually Sam started his car and drove off into the night. He felt far better, as he drove, than when he had picked Cheryl up. He knew he had not lost Cheryl.

Sam called Cheryl every night that week letting her know how much he loved her. All that week he struggled with what he was going to do. The thought of hurting his wife and abandoning his marriage and son was something that he was finding a very hard thing to do. The next time Sam was with Cheryl it was much less emotional and so much calmer and happier for them. As they kept on seeing each other, not as often as before because his wife was taking a much tougher stand, it was almost if nothing had changed for them,. What were they going to do about Cheryl being pregnant though? Sam, like always, procrastinating wanting dearly to get back to the life he had with Cheryl before. It would be awhile before Cheryl was to have her baby, so he though he had time, and he believed he was getting closer to telling his wife he was going to leave her, but he still could not do it. He kept telling Cheryl he would leave his wife and he really believed he was going to.

Weeks later Sam while on a date with Cheryl was feeling so good, with things back to the way they were, and with his love sitting so close beside him when she said something, very matter of factly; to break the wonderful spell he was in. "Sam I've decided to get an abortion." So very shocked, Sam almost didn't know what to say, it took him awhile to collect his thoughts. Cheryl aborting their child had been something that he had not even considered. So he finally turned to her and said, "Cheryl, you can't have an abortion. I'm going to leave my wife and then we can get married. I want to be the father of our baby. Cheryl then said, sounding very sure of herself, "Sam, you're not going to leave your wife." He knew that she could be right, but he really did feel that he was going to leave her, but he had not, so he said, "Cheryl, I have no right to tell you not to have an abortion after what I have done, and not leaving my wife, but I do want to be our baby's father and marry you and I will. Don't abort our baby Cheryl."

"You shouldn't leave you wife and child Sam. I will be alright."

"I hear it could be dangerous."

"I'm going to have it done by a doctor at a clinic. It's very safe Sam." Then sounding very tired she continued. "Please, Sam, I don't want to talk about it." Although Sam wanted to continue to convince her not to have the abortion, he knew he did not have that right, and knew by the way she sounded she would not listen anyway, and did not want to listen. He didn't want to have his baby killed and for Cheryl to go through an abortion, but he could tell that she truly had made up her mind to do it. The abortion stayed on his mind the whole night even after he had taken her home and was on his way to Crescent and long after that. He felt it made him even more likely that he would tell his wife he was going to leave her, to save their baby, as he continued to get closer to doing that.

Sam continued to see Cheryl almost every weekend. He no longer was trying very hard to hide the fact that he was seeing Cheryl, from his wife. He would make up some dumb excuse whenever he went to see her, most of the time just saying he was going drinking with his friends at the Tavern, and he would be back later. He was beginning to want her to know what he was doing, and feeling for sure that she did know what was going on, but she would say nothing.

One day, though, she did look through his billfold and found a little piece of scrap paper. The small piece of paper Cheryl had written her name and phone number on, with her eye liner pencil, at the Greenwood the night he met her. Sam had never thrown it away, but he was to wish he had. Brenda was far from her family and the only friends she had were Sam's family so she was feeling very alone when she thought she was going to lose him. When she found the paper with the name and the number on it she knew exactly what it was so she boldly called the number written on it. Cheryl answered the phone and then Brenda said. "Is this Cheryl?" Sounding a little puzzled because she did not recognize the voice she answered, "Yes, this is Cheryl."

"My name is Brenda Jackson I think you know my husband, Sam." Cheryl was no longer puzzled and after a second answered honestly, "Yes, I know Sam."

"Well I found your phone number in his billfold and wondered what it was doing there. I think you have been seeing my husband. Have you been?"

"Yes I have, but I didn't know he was married until recently."

"I don't know if he told you, but we have a little boy.'

"Yes, I know, Sam told me about your son when he told me he was married." Then she demanded,

"Well, I want you to quit seeing my husband because he is married to me and I love him and his son loves him and needs him." Cheryl felt sympathy for Brenda, but she would not give up Sam so she said, "I think it's up to Sam. If he wants to stop seeing me he can anytime he wants."

"Do you love Sam?"

"Yes, I love him." Then Brenda starting crying before she said, "Well I want you to stop seeing my husband and let him come back to me and our son." Then she hung up and continued crying alone. That evening Brenda said nothing when Sam made his usual excuse and left her alone. She did not try to keep him home like she had been doing lately. Sam thought as he left that she had been unusually quiet that evening. When Sam picked up Cheryl, he felt she acted a little cool towards him also. After they had driven a few miles in silence she said, "Brenda called me today." Sam turned quickly to look at Cheryl and sounding worried said, "How did she get your number?"

"She said she found on a piece of paper in your billfold."

"Dam; I never threw away that piece of paper that you wrote your phone number down on, when I first met you." Sam was mad thinking that Brenda might have jeopardized his relationship with Cheryl and not even worried that she now knew about Cheryl. "I should have thrown it away a long time ago."

"Yes you should have." Sam thought Cheryl might be angry and maybe even not want to see him anymore. He could tell that she was not, though, as she calmly said, "She said she wanted me to leave you alone because you are married to her and needed to take care of your little boy. She never sounded angry, but she wants me to leave you alone." Sam thought that Cheryl seemed to be feeling sympathy for Brenda. That was alright with him as long as she did not leave him. He was determined to stop talking about Brenda, though, and felt after what she had done, it was even more likely than ever that he would leave her, or she would leave him. It seemed to Sam that Cheryl did not want to talk about the phone call any more than he did because she did not say another word about it. She just put her arm around him and watched the passing scenery on the way to their favorite parking spot in the hills.

After Sam parked the car Cheryl had some more news for him. Sam, my brother's got a new job in Portland at Saint Anthony's Hospital. He's going to be head of the personnel department. He and Nancy are going to move up their next week. "Sam's mood had quickly changed to a deep despair. After all he had gone through he was going to lose her anyway. "You're going to move back to Portland?"

"Yes, I'd stay here if I could, but I don't know anybody I could stay with in Springfield. Sam, you know that I don't want to leave you, but I have to. Next weekend the movers will be moving Nancy's things and then she will be leaving and I have to leave with her. I will be living in an apartment with them until they find a house up there. Nancy and I will be packing up her things all this week. Sam did not want to believe his ears and was now thoroughly depressed, but sounding determined he said, I'm going home right now and tell Brenda I'm going to leave her."

"Sam I don't want you to do that. We can still see each other. Portland is only a three hour drive. You took me to Portland, for the day, last month you know it's not that far. I'm going to get me a job and come down and see you."

"I won't be able to see you enough though."

"It won't be bad Sam."

"Yes, it will" Cheryl continued to sound upbeat especially compared to Sam as he said; "I will divorce my wife. I will and you'll live in Crescent with me. We'll get married."

"Sam, you love you're wife you know it. We will see each other." She was leaving him for sure now, so Sam was wondering why she was not as upset about it as he was, did she truly just want things to go along as they had been with them. "But not enough. I want to see you all the time I want us to get married."

"I know, Sam, but we can't" Sounding desperate Sam said, "I know what we'll do. I have some money in the Credit Union. It's not a lot but it's enough get you a room for awhile until you get a job in Springfield."

"Sam how am I going to look for work? I don't have a car." Then she slowly let a small smile crease her face as she said, "I like the idea of being a kept woman, though." That answer, and her little smile, caused Sam mood to lighten, and a smile to also appear on his face which he tried to repress but couldn't as Cheryl continued, "If you were rich you could find me a fancy apartment and I could be your kept woman." Sam now with a big smile glad the tenseness for him was over said, "Yes, you could be my mistress." They were both feeling much better now especially Sam who had felt, and acted like he was losing her forever. He knew that he shouldn't have worried because Cheryl was right they would still see each other maybe as much as they always had. Cheryl had defused his worry and they then made love with the greater passion that they had found since almost losing each other.

During the next week Sam was able to get away a couple of times to see Cheryl keeping his energy at work and at night with some of the little white crosses Cheryl provided for him as he started using them more often. Brenda didn't say anything about her call to Cheryl and Sam said nothing, so they went on living much like they had always done before. Neither of them wanting to deal with what they knew they would have to deal with eventually.

On the Saturday the day before she was to leave for Portland as they nestled in their mountain top retreat, Cheryl told him. "Sam, I'm going to stay at my sister-in-law Jackie's while I'm in Portland. We have always been good friends. She is the one that is divorced from my brother the one that lives in the houseboat. I get along great with her, her new husband, and my two nephews. I've lived with them before." Then she smiled and said, "They like me. I don't know why but they do. I didn't even have to ask her if I could stay. She asked me. You'll be able to call me there and visit any time you want. She knows all about you and I know you will like her."

"I don't know anything about Portland. I'll never be able to find her house."

"Sam, Portland is an easy place to get around. You won't have any problem. When you get up there you can call me and I can give you directions. It is easy to find."

"Okay, I'll come up tomorrow."

"Sam, you're not going to come up to Portland tomorrow are you?"

"Yes, you know I can't stay away from you."

"It's too soon Sam. I'm going to be at my mother's house until Thursday."

"Dam! You mean I won't be able to see you until next weekend?"

"Yes, next week if you are able to come. We can spend the whole weekend together if you want."

"Don't you worry, I'll be there for sure, but that's to long to be away from you."

"I guess you do love me?"

"Yep." That night Sam kissed her like always before leaving her at her door. He was feeling much better, but still did not like knowing that she was going to be so far away from him, but Cheryl had completely eased his mind about her living in Portland.

Chapter Eight
A Terrible Night

The week after Cheryl had gone to Portland was a bad week for Sam. He had not lost her forever, but that week it almost felt like it to him. Early in the week he hardly talked to Brenda and didn't play with Patrick as much as usual. He knew that Brenda was wondering what he was going to say about her calling Cheryl. She was acting nervous around him and seemed to be watching and waiting for him to say something. He didn't want to say anything. He just wished she had not found out about Cheryl. After being there at home that whole week, with his wife and child, and so far away from Cheryl, and not calling her, he started feeling more like a part of his family again. As he had thought before he started thinking that he shouldn't see Cheryl again, and never should have started seeing her in the first place, complicating his life, and that he should never have keep on seeing her, and then to fall in love with her, and to have sex with her, and then to not expect her to get pregnant. He knew though that he was crazy in love with her and would not just throw her away even though he still loved his wife and child, and wanted to do the right thing by them. He continued to wrestle with what to do about it. He was feeling much more pressure now that Cheryl was pregnant even if she said she was going to have an abortion. At the end of the week on Friday, Sam was sitting with Brenda watching television after putting Patrick to sleep. With it being the time that he usually was going to see Cheryl he was slowly getting angry with Brenda blaming her for keeping him from Cheryl. His feelings being agitated by the fact that the new car he had bought was broken down and was the real reason that was keeping him from going to Portland. He was still thinking though that if it wasn't for Brenda he'd be seeing Cheryl that weekend. Deep down he knew he was being unfair, but he let the thought take hold of him anyway. The more he sat there and thought about it the more he believed he would be able to do what had been impossible for him to do up until then. He did not want to hurt Brenda but now he felt there was no way out of it. So he turned to her and calmly in a lowered voice said, "Brenda I know you looked in my billfold last week and you found a phone number and called it." Brenda turned her head quickly to look at him with a look of fear on her face. She at first just stared at him saying nothing. Although he had asked her with determination he felt fear himself for he knew what a fateful decision he was making. He was destroying his marriage and breaking his commitment to Brenda and Patrick. He was being a heel and he knew his family and friends would think him one because they all liked Brenda. He was also leaving his son behind, although he knew that he would stay in his life. Brenda said defiantly, "Yes, I found a number with a girls name on it. I called the number and talked to your girlfriend, who I know you have been seeing for a long time. All those times you left us by ourselves. You have not fooled me. I called her to tell her to leave you alone; you have not, though, have you? You're my husband and I love you and need you. You have a son to take care of. I want her to leave you alone." Sam watched her, feeling her pain for he loved her still, but he also had started feeling detached from her because he was determined to be with Cheryl and he knew he could not let his feelings for Brenda stop him. After she had finished talking she continued to stare at him trying to read his face. With determination again showing on his face, and feeling detached from his feelings for her he said, "Brenda, I love you but I love Cheryl more. I want a divorce so that I can marry her." Brenda, shocking Sam, with a look of horror on her face, suddenly howled at the top of her lungs as loud and long as she could. When she had finished she yelled in his face, "I won't let you have a divorce! You can't do it Sam! You have to take care of Patrick, and you have to stay with me. Then she collapsed back onto her cushioned chair to cry and moan as loud as she had before.

Sam had never expected her to take it the way she was. She would not stop her loud howling as she continued on loud and long. Sam had felt bad about telling her he was leaving her, and her wailing was making him feel ten time's worse. She ran from her chair over to the couch and lay their sobbing. Sam, feeling terrible and wanting so bad to comfort her, scooted over on the couch to hold her and she let him as the tears ran down her cheeks and onto his shirt. She allowed him to hold her as she clung to him very tightly and continued to yell. As the night wore on she never wavered in the loudness of her crying or in the tightness of her hold on Sam, making him feel worse and worse. He expected her to be hurt and angry, but not the constant wailing that Sam knew the neighbors had to be able to hear through the thin apartment walls. As the wetness of her tears soaked his shoulder he held her, rocking her back and forth through the night hour after hour. Sometimes he would tell that he would always love her, but that just caused her to cry louder. He felt so bad that he just wanted to tell her that he would not leave her so that she would not cry anymore. That night brought back the feelings of love that he had felt for her when they were first married, and oh how he did love her then. He had thought as the years of their marriage went by that she did not love him as much as he loved her, or that she even really loved him at all. She was showing him just how much she did love him with her hours of crying. He wondered why she hadn't shown him this great love before. As the wailing continued after midnight it made Sam wonder if he had made the right decision as all that early love for her continued flowing back to him. He was feeling so bad for the girl that he had married and made his wife, and had loved so much, and still loved so much, as she cried on and on. He had wondered if she truly loved him and now he knew, as he rocked her past two O'clock and even later in the morning. He was feeling so bad that he knew that it had to be the worst night of his life. His heart continued to ache for Brenda as she cried and cried. He was starting to feel something he had no idea he would feel just hours earlier. He was beginning to feel that he was going to stay with Brenda his wife and the mother of his son. The woman he had promised his life to. That was how he was feeling when Brenda finally quieted at about three in the morning. The two of them then got up and without a word trudged down the hall to the bedroom, where totally exhausted they feel into bed to fall asleep.

Sam woke late the next morning to the sounds of Brenda opening the dresser drawer. As Sam adjusted to the morning light he could see that she was completely dressed and had an open suitcase lying on the floor filled with her cloths. Behind her he could see Patrick all dressed watching his mother fill her suitcase. Brenda's attitude had changed completely. There were no tears now, just a determined look on her face as she continued to fill her suitcase. Very surprised Sam sat up and blurted out, "Where are you going?"

"I called Mike and Jean this morning and they'll be here in two hours to pick up Patrick and me." Sam was so completely surprised that he was dumbfounded. He knew that she would be going home to her folks, but he thought it would be a least a day or two, maybe even a week, before she left with Patrick. He had forgotten about Mike and Jean from Portland. Mike had come from the same little town that Brenda had been raised in, and was friends of her and her family. Sam stayed in bed trying to focus his mind and trying to think of what to do. He had decided the night before that he was going to stay with Brenda, after her night of crying, but the firm look of determination on her face and with the plans she had already made he knew he could not stop her now. He had to live with what he had done, at least for now. As he put his cloths on he asked Brenda in a resigned tone of voice, "You're going to have to take some money out of the checking account to buy the plane ticket." Brenda sounding very businesslike said, "Mike and Jean have bought me a ticket and I have already written out a check to pay them back." Then she just went on with her packing. Sam was already feeling lonely as he watched her finish her packing. He played with Patrick forcing a smile on his face knowing it would be a long time before he would see him again. Thoughts of Cheryl, who had filled his mind, were gone as he waited for Brenda and Patrick's ride that would take them away from him. Brenda soon had all her clothes packed, and everything else she was taking in the front room ready to go. The three of them sat and waited with Sam holding Patrick on his knee. Brenda sat with a very firm look on her face saying nothing, and not looking at Sam. Patrick feeling the tension in the room looked back and forth at his mom and dad with a look of unhappiness on his face. After sitting there quietly for awhile Sam finally said, "Have you called your folks?" Brenda let her guard down a little said softly, Yes, I called them this morning before I called Mike and Jean. My father was the one who told me to call them." They were going to pay for my ticket, but I told them we had enough money." Just then they heard a car drive up in front of the apartment. Brenda went immediately to the front door and opened it just as Jean was getting to the door. Brenda ran to her and hugged her in a long and tight embrace. Then she gave Mike a hug. Sam stood back watching them feeling very uncomfortable and guilty. He carried Brenda's suitcases to the car and helped Mike load them, without saying a word, not breaking the mood of sadness. After he was finished, he picked; up Patrick to kiss him on the cheek, and tell him that he loved him. He gave him to Brenda who took him without looking at Sam. When she had put him in the car and went to get in herself Sam said, "I'll write to you Brenda." She then closed her door and Sam watched them drive away with tears welling in his eyes. After they had disappeared from sight he slowly walked back into his very quiet and lonely apartment and sat down in the darkness of the room. There he sat for hour after lonely hour thinking of what a mess he had made of his life.

CHAPTER NINE
TOGETHER AGAIN

Sam finally pulled himself up from the couch on that fateful day that his family left him. He slowly walked down the hall to lie in his bed, which now seemed so big without Brenda beside him. It wasn't even dark when he lay down to sleep and he hadn't eaten all day, but he didn't care. He tried to sleep but could not. He was very troubled by the loneliness that he felt with Brenda and Patrick gone, and how they were now maybe lost to him forever.

He remembered vividly the preceding night. That long, terrible night he held Brenda as she cried so loud and so long as his heart ached for her. He truly felt that was the worst night of his life seeing and hearing her hurt so terribly. It had made him want to go back to her and make that terrible night up to her. As he laid there he also thought about the reason he wanted to leave her. It was Cheryl and his love for her. It had taken him such a long time to make up his mind to leave Brenda. He had gone through so much turmoil that he knew he had to give his relationship with Cheryl a chance and he also loved her so very much. Around midnight Sam, worn out from worry, finally fell asleep.

Late the next morning when he got out of bed, Sam was still feeling very sad and lonely. He was going to call Cheryl and he knew that just talking to her would make him feel much better. After he ate his breakfast he dialed the number she had given him and soon heard her voice. "Cheryl, it's so good to hear your voice. It seems like it's been so long since I've heard it."

"Sam! It's only been a week."

"I know, but it seems longer. I've missed you."

"I've missed you Sam."

"Would it be all right if I came to Portland to see you today? I'd really like to see you." He hadn't wanted to because he would have to use his brother's car, since his car had broken down, and because he had been using his brother's car a lot he didn't want to use it again. There was no way he was going to stay away from Cheryl that day, though, even if he had to hitch hike, but he knew his brother would lend his car to him, even if he wasn't very happy about it. "Yes, Sam you can come on up. I'm not doing a thing. I haven't a thing on my schedule, but can you get away from you wife?"

"I can get away anytime I want to now."

"What, do you mean Sam?"

"I did what you never thought I would do, I left my wife." Astonished, Cheryl blurted out, "You left your wife?" Sam calmly answered, "Yes, Brenda left yesterday. Some friends from Portland came and picked her and Patrick up."

"Sam, are you telling me the truth?"

"Yes, Cheryl, I told Brenda Friday night I wanted a divorce. She called home and to her friends early Saturday morning, and by noon she and Patrick were gone. Now they are a thousand miles away."

"Sam you shouldn't have. You shouldn't have left your family."

"I know Cheryl and I miss them, but I love you and I can't wait to be with you."

"I know Sam but I didn't want you to break up your family."

"It's to late Cheryl, I've already done it. Brenda is with her family. There is no turning back now." Sam had expected Cheryl to be very surprised at the news, but he had expected her to be happier about him leaving Brenda than she acted, although she did seem to be happy. Then the question that he had wanted to ask ever since he had called her, he asked her. Will you come down here and live with me now. How I would love to see you every day instead of just now and then like I do now. Then only half kidding he said, "You're not going to leave me now that I've left my wife are you?"

"No Sam! You know I won't leave you."

"Then when I come to Portland can I pick you up and bring you down here to live with me? Cheryl I really need you. I'm so lonely now."

"Yes, Sam I'll come down, but only for a week. I promised my sister I would help her move the following week."

"That's alright; at least I'll have you for a week." Now anxious he said. "I'll leave as soon as I can. I should be there in a little over three hours. I'll call you when I get there for directions."

"Okay Sam. I'll be waiting for your call." Sam hung up the phone and hurried to borrow his brother's car so he could be on his way. He soon was on the road and getting that great feeling that he always got when he was on his way to see Cheryl. He felt especially good after feeling so depressed. Time on the trip went by fast for Sam even thought the ride from Crescent to Portland is very long and mostly straight and boring. Sam had thoughts of seeing Cheryl to keep his mind occupied though. He drove mile after mile in a happy trance with thoughts of Cheryl. Brenda and Patrick were pushed far aside in his mind as he hurried on his way to Cheryl.

After arriving in Portland he made his call and was given directions, and was soon on one of the many very long bridges, which arch high over the Willamette River in Portland. The river, at the point where Sam was crossing it in Portland was on its way to meet the very wide and deep Columbia River and when the two joined they made a huge river that soon emptied into the Pacific Ocean. As he climbed higher and higher on the bridge the tall skyscrapers of the main part of town, with high green hills in the background, were on his left. The rest of the sprawling city was to his right. He looked far down at the river at the large ships docked on the dark blue river below. He did not look long though thinking it would be a very long fall to the cold blue river below if he drove off that bridge. The big city had always been a curiosity to him. He always liked to drive between the tall skyscrapers in the middle of the city where people crowded the streets. There was an excitement for him that he did not get in his part of the world.

Sam had soon crossed the bridge and was to find it was much easier to find Cheryl than he thought it would be. After a few miles of leaving the bridge he was turning at the exit where Cheryl had told him to turn. Then, after, a few more blocks, he turned onto, what he thought, was one of the main arteries through town. Stores and businesses, with some of them boarded up, lined the sides of the road. He was not on that road very long before he turned off into a residential neighborhood and soon found the house that held Cheryl. It was a thirty-year old single story wooden house with a porch whose roof was held up by large square pillars. It looked much like the house Sam was raised in and his mother and step-father still resided in. The street, the house sat on, also looked much the same as Sam's old street. It didn't have the huge old trees that lined the street that he grew up on, the large old Walnut trees, Maple trees, and the Cherry tree that stood in front of his old home. The yards were much too small for huge trees.

Sam walked up to the pale yellow house with brown trim around it's windows, and climbed the steps onto the porch. He nervously rang the door bell. The door was open, just the screen door was closed. In the back of the house Sam heard a female voice yell, "Someone get the door!" Then looking through the screen, Sam could see a thin young boy who must have been about ten years old, come shyly up to the door. As he walked up, Sam said, "Hi is Cheryl Thompson here?" They boy then softly said, "Yes."

"Could you tell her that Sam Jackson is here to see her?" The boy turned quickly and ran off yelling, "Cheryl there is somebody at the door for you. Somebody named Sam." Cheryl appeared at the door then with her sister-in-law beside her. Cheryl looked happy to see him, which made him feel good. She quickly invited him in and introduced him to Jackie and her two sons, Cheryl's nephews. Jackie reminded Sam of the singer Cher. She had long straight black hair and was thin with a long pretty face like the singer, and even had her deep voice. Cheryl held her suitcase, which Sam liked because he was not good at small talk with people he didn't know. Cheryl made her farewells and was soon sitting beside him and they were on their way to Crescent to live together. Sam felt so great because he had been dreaming of her living with him for so long, and now it was finally going to be a reality. Her attitude towards him since he had first seen her through the screen door had taken away his doubt that she wanted to be with him. She had been so happy to see him and still seemed happy to be sitting there beside him. It lifted his spirits when he felt her soft warm body as she snuggled up close to him.

Cheryl turned to him as they drove on and happily said, "Sam I can't believe that you told your wife that you wanted to leave her."

"But I did." Then turning to her he said, "Because I love you."

"Yes I know Sam but you shouldn't have done it. I know you love your wife and child, and they need you."

"Cheryl, you know that I cannot live without you. You're going to be my wife. I told you we were going to get married and we are. You didn't believe me when I told you I was going to marry you, did you?"

"No, Sam, I didn't and I didn't think you would."

"So, I should take you back to Sandy's then?"

"No! Sam I'm coming with you wherever you want to take me." Sam had no doubt then that she was his. She then squeezed closer to him and the car became quiet as Sam put his arm around her, and held her tightly. As they continued driving through Portland on their way to Crescent they were happy to be together without either of them saying a word. Sam thought of how their world had changed so very much in just two days, and how she would soon be truly living with him. As they neared the exit to Salem, Oregon's capital city, Cheryl turned to Sam and calmly and conversationally said, Sam I got an abortion last Wednesday." Sam was so very surprised. He had not expected her to have the abortion so soon. He did not answer her right away. He had not wanted her to get an abortion and kill their child so he sat there driving quietly staring ahead, feeling very sad and guilty that she had gone through with the abortion. He had thought that after leaving Brenda, they would raise their child. He knew it was his fault, though, because if he'd left Brenda sooner he would have saved their child. Like always, it seemed, he procrastinated and this time it cost the life of his child. Before in Hendricks Park when she first told him, he knew he had no right to tell her not to have an abortion and he had no right to tell her it was wrong now. Since Sam said nothing, Cheryl continued, Danny went with me." Sam was glad that she had not been alone. He knew that as independent as she was, that she would have gone alone if she had to. He had been surprised that Danny had been the one to go with her though. She continued, "I had the appointment for the abortion in the middle of the day and Danny was the only one that could get off work to go with me. Listening to Cheryl he wished he had been the one to go with her or better for her not to have had one at all. "We took the bus down to the clinic and Danny stayed in the waiting room until they were finished. After I came out I was a littler woozy and he was so sweet taking my arm and helping me walk, and helping all the way home and worrying about me the whole time. Sam finally said, "I'm glad that Danny was with you. You needed to have someone with you. I wish that I could have been there for you."

"Sam, I'm a big girl. I can take care of myself."

"I know, but I still wish I could have been there." Sam sad and not wanting to talk about the abortion any more said nothing more about it and neither did Cheryl. As the evening grew dimmer Sam turned the headlights on as he drove on in the quiet car with Cheryl continuing to lean on him.

He had thoughts of how much she must truly love him after what he had done, and how the two of them had made such a tremendous break from their past lives to be with each other. With Sam's arm around Cheryl, holding her close and with her head on his shoulder he could not help but think of the happiness that was ahead of them. He had made a great leap but he had to give them a chance. He was starting his life all over again and leaving his family, but he would now have Cheryl all to himself. She would be waiting for him every night when he came home from work. Finally Sam pulled his car into the parking lot of his apartment building, in Crescent, and he and Cheryl were soon in their new home. Tired they went right to sleep lying together in each other's arms.

The next morning, Sam's alarm went off at five o'clock rousing him and Cheryl from their sleep. Sam immediately jumped to his feet and started throwing on his cloths. Cheryl sat up in the bed, yawned and said sleepily, "Do you want me to fix you breakfast?"

"No, I don't eat breakfast but you can make me a sandwich for lunch if you want." She got out of bed and padded drowsily down the carpeted hall to turn right at the end of it to enter the kitchen. Sam finished putting on his work cloths and grabbed his cork boots and followed her down the hall. In the kitchen, Cheryl started going through the kitchen cabinets until she saw Sam then she asked, "Where is the bread?"

"It's in that top right cabinet in front of you."

"What do you want in your sandwich?"

"I think there is some ham and cheese in the refrigerator. Just put mayonnaise and mustard on it." Sam was getting a kick out of seeing

Cheryl in his kitchen. It was so different or surreal, but he had dreamed about living with her so often. She was really right there in front of him in person and real as could be. He could not help but smile watching her put his sandwich together. He tore himself away from his wonderful thoughts so he could grab a snack cake and an orange. He put them in his metal lunch box, along with the sandwich Cheryl had made him, and snapped it shut. They waited, sitting together on the couch, both of them half asleep and leaning on each other. Soon the headlights of the Crummy lit up the blinds on the big window in front of the apartment. Sam rose and picked up his cork boots and lunch pail. Cheryl stood by to kiss him, and then he was out the door and into the Crummy. Climbing to the back seat Sam lay across it with a little smile on his face because he was feeling so good thinking about coming home to Cheryl.

The day went fast for Sam with a little help from a little white cross that Cheryl had given him, and him thinking about coming home to her. All the logs were easy for him to set his choker on that day. He was in a good mood and so it seemed was every one else, even Boney seemed content and not on edge ready to snap like he often was, but Sam always excused Boney, knowing it was his equipment and there were many things that could go wrong if he wasn't on top of things. If he wasn't' sending logs down the road he wouldn't be making money, and he needed a lot of cash just to make the payments on the big Yarder, and Loader sitting there on the landing, not to mention the payroll for the crew. Sam was still feeling great when he got home that night for his first evening at home with Cheryl. She was at the stove cooking supper when he grabbed her around the waist hugging and lifting her to swing her around the kitchen and yelling, "It's so great to see you here finally."

"Stop it you're getting me dirty. Take off those dirty cloths and take a shower.

"Okay but I'll be back soon."

"Hurry supper's about ready." Then as soon as he took his hot shower, washing the dirt off from a hard day's work, his supper was ready for him. They sat down to their first meal together in their home. Cheryl said as she sat down at the table. "Sam you don't have a lot of groceries, but I put together what I could."

"Yea, I know, we didn't buy any groceries last week. We were going to buy them Friday, but that's when I told Brenda that I was going to leave her. It took all our grocery money for her to buy the plane tickets so we're going to have to scrimp until Friday when I get paid. We can go tonight and get a few groceries my car should be finished being worked on." So what Sam got that night for his first supper with Cheryl was macaroni and a small hamburger patty. That was alright with him, though, because he got to eat it with Cheryl, and later that night he got to make love to her not in the back seat of a car but in a real bed. That week went along about the same, skimpy meals but wonderful nights in bed. There were times though, even when he was there with Cheryl, that he would miss playing with his little boy. He could not keep those thoughts out of his mind, even his thoughts of Brenda. With Cheryl living with him, though, he could always hold her and know how much he had wanted her right there with him where she was.'

CHAPTER TEN
THAT RAINY NIGHT

Wednesday night of the week that Cheryl had came to live with Sam; Cheryl told Sam, "Do you remember that I've got to help my sister move this Friday?"

"Yes, I remember." Sam said grudgingly. "Tomorrow, Mandy is coming to pick me up at around seven in the morning so I won't be here tomorrow when you get off work." Sam looked at Cheryl, then smiled widely and pleaded, "Are you sure you have to go? You know that you will be leaving me all by my self don't you?"

"I'm sorry, Sam, but Mandy is only going to have me help her. So I've got to go."

"What about her husband, Pete?"

"He is going to be away for a week. He is a salesman like my brother Danny so he is gone often." Sam sure wasn't looking forward to being without Cheryl, especially when they had just started living together. He knew that there was no talking her out of it, though, because she sounded so determined. So Sam resigned himself to the fact that she was leaving. That night, they went to bed and made wonderful love, with Sam knowing it would have to last him for awhile.

When Sam got home from work the next evening, to his surprise Cheryl was still there. She was in the kitchen getting his supper ready and he was happy thinking that she was not leaving. He could tell she was agitated as she walked quickly around the kitchen while she cooked supper, not saying a word to him, not even looking at him as he stood watching her at the entrance to the kitchen. After he showered and came back into the kitchen, she had settled down a little so she said to him, "Mandy can't come and get me because her car broke down yesterday. She has it in the shop for repairs."

"That's too bad. I know how much you wanted to help your sister." Of course Sam wasn't sorry at all. In fact he was feeling very happy that she would have to stay with him for the weekend, but then Cheryl said, "Sam but I've decided to hitchhike up there after we eat supper. A shocked Sam hesitated and then raised his voice as he said, "Cheryl you can't hitchhike up there! It's not safe and it's going to be dark soon. Nobody picks people up after dark. A girl hitchhiking at night would just be asking for trouble. If they weren't still working on my car, I could give you a ride, and my brother I know won't let me borrow his car again, but there is no way that I'm going to let you hitchhike up there tonight."

"Sam you can't stop me. I'll be alright. I've hitchhiked lots of times."

"Have you ever hitchhiked at night?"

"No, but I will be alright Sam. "Then looking very stern she said. "I'm going and you cannot stop me." Sam had never seen her so determined before. For the first time she didn't seem to care what he thought and he knew for sure she was going to go. He was truly afraid for her, though, so he said, "If you have to go, then I'm going with you."

"Sam, you can't come with me you have to work in the morning."

"I know so after I hitchhike up there with you; I'll just turn around and hitchhike back."

"Sam you can't do that. You'll never make it back in time to catch the Crummy for work."

"I think I can make it. I should have plenty of time to make it. Sam was just as determined as Cheryl. He did not think that Cheryl thought he was really going to go with her though, but when they finished supper and Cheryl walked out the door to start hitchhiking Sam was right behind her. He was just not going to let her go by herself. He knew it was not safe for her.

It had been raining off and on all day as it often does in Western Oregon in November. It had made it a very wet and muddy day for Sam at work, but he was used to it, staying warm by working hard thus warming himself, and keeping his body heat from escaping by wearing a rubber coat and pants. As they started walking quickly down the sidewalk, there was a slight mist in the air that wetted and cooled their cheeks. Everything around them was soaked from a recent rain. The big dark trees whose limbs reached out over their heads dropped big drops of cold water on their heads and shoulders causing them to shiver each time the drops hit.

The grasses in the lawns they passed were thick with beads of water that shown like diamonds as they reflected the light from the street lights and the gutters on the sides of the streets were filled with rushing water. The streets looked like they were covered with shiny black ice with the light from the streetlights shining off their surfaces.

They were two very lonely figures as they rushed on, almost running along the sidewalks beside the very empty streets. The streetlights were making eerie halos high in the dark sky above them, and shining down on their glistening faces, as they hurried down Sixth Street to Quincy then east to Tenth Street. They walked diagonally across many streets named after long dead presidents to the city park. There they walked under the tall trees in the Park, which looked eerie with the bright lights shining up into them in the dark night. By then they were glad for the cold mist that was falling on them, because their cheeks were hot from the exertion of walking across town so quickly. Once out of the park, they waked along the sidewalks out of town, up a slow incline as they followed east Main Street. That was when it started raining in earnest pouring down heavily on them. When they got to where Main Street ran under Interstate Five, they climbed up a muddy bank and onto the highway. There, in the pouring rain, they huddled together sticking their thumbs out and watching the dim lights of the cars get brighter as they approached and then whizzed by them. The Interstate was busy that very dark and wet night and every car that passed would spay gusts of ice cold water on the two solitary figures, beside the road, making them even wetter and colder. From the beginning, Sam hoped that they would not be able to get a ride so they would have to go back to the apartment. Now that they were on the highway and getting rained on, and soaked by the spray from the cars that passed, he wanted even more for Cheryl to give up so they could go back to the warm and dry apartment. As they watched car after car pass them it looked like he was going to get his wish. He knew though that because Cheryl had been so very insistent on going that she would not give up easily. He was finding out just how tough and determined she was as they continued to stay there on the side of the road after they were drenched. Sam was used to working out in the cold rain and getting soaking wet. Cheryl was not, but she was giving no indication of giving up. Sam did not understand why she was so insistent, and willing to go through such an ordeal, but there was no way that he was going to let her go by herself. He knew how unsafe it could be for her, but Cheryl certainly didn't seem to believe she was being unsafe or she didn't care acting tough like she often did.

At first Sam and Cheryl stayed out near the road so it would be easy for the speeding cars to see them and give them a ride. Both of them were taking the full force of the wind and water that the cars sprayed on them pushing them away from the edge of the road. Sam soon had Cheryl, who was wearing only her thin blue denim coat, stand back from the road. He wanted to protect her from the ice cold spray coming from the passing cars. Sam had on his light jacket, the only good coat he owned, and it was already soaked through, but he was used to being wet and cold. This time though he was not working hard in his rubber coat which would have kept him dryer and trapped his body heat. Sam stayed out on the edge of the road; sticking out his thumb taking the full brunt of the cold wind and spray. As Sam stayed there and got colder and wetter, he began to think that he would have to give up before he froze to death, the icy spray was actually causing him pain each time it splashed him. He thought he was tough but he was freezing. He knew though that there was no way that he would let her go to Portland by herself, so he forced himself to stay where he was and continued to freeze. After awhile though he seemed to get numb to the cold and it became easier for him to take even the force of the spray from the big eighteen wheelers that would move him back away from the road with the force of their spray. Then, to Sam's dismay, a car stopped. He thought as he watched it slow down and stop that at least they were getting out of the cold and rain and near a heater. Sam and Cheryl ran up the road to the late model red mustang. When they got there, Sam opened the passenger door. The girl driver yelled out to them. "Hi guys. Where are you going?"

"We're going to Portland." Sam answered back. "Get in then. I can take you most of the way. I'm going to Oregon City." As she lay back the passenger seat so Sam could climb into the back seat. She said, "Just move those suitcases over." Sam piled the two suitcases on top of each other then sat down in the back seat and said, "Thanks for stopping. Sorry we're getting your car so wet but we are soaked." The girl answered as Cheryl climbed into the front passenger seat. "That's alright the water won't hurt anything. I'm a student from Southern Oregon College and I'm going home to Oregon City for the weekend" She then drove back onto the wet highway with Sam and Cheryl loving being out of the cold and rain and felling the heat from the car's heater. Soon after they had driven back onto the highway the girl said, "What are your names? Mine is Betty Adams." Cheryl then said. "My name is Cheryl Peterson and that is Sam Jackson in the back seat."

"Glad to meet you. What are you guys doing out in this rain hitchhiking?"

"We need to get to Portland tonight. Sam's car is not running so we decided to hitchhike." Said, Cheryl quickly. Then Sam broke in, "How is Southern Oregon? I used to go there. It's been quite a while though. It's been about four years. I was only there for two years."

"How come you stopped?"

"I got drafted into the Army and after I got out I just never went back."

""You should have it's a great place."

"Maybe someday I will." Then the car was quiet for a while as the girl drove on. After driving for a few miles she asked Sam if he would drive, saying that she was tired and falling asleep. Sam had noticed that she was driving slower than the rest of the traffic as car after car had passed her. He thought she might be afraid of driving at night in the heavy rain, and had been watching her driving closely, as had Cheryl. He never dreamed that she would let him, a stranger, drive her great looking Mustang though. Sam was sure the Mustang was one of the more expensive models with the big motor and all the extras. He gladly accepted her invitation to drive. Sam changed seats with the girl and she quickly went to sleep in the back seat. Sam drove much faster than the girl had. He certainly wasn't afraid of driving in the rain. Driving in Oregon he had lots of experience driving in the rain. Sam drove faster but he did not drive faster than the speed limit after all it was not his car. He did wish that he could have really tested the powerful car though. One reason he was glad he was driving because now that they were going faster he would get to Portland sooner and then he would have a better chance to get back to his apartment before the Crummy showed up.

As they neared Portland, Sam was tempted not to take the Oregon City turn off like the sleeping girl surely wanted him to do. He knew that she could get to Oregon City from Portland and it would not be that much farther for her to travel. As they approached the Oregon City exit, though, Sam turned off onto the exit and did what he knew was right. He drove on towards Oregon City, but stopped before they got there to wake up Betty. They had arrived at the highway that ran between Oregon City and Portland. She then took the highway to Oregon City and Sam and Cheryl started hitchhiking in the opposite direction. Thankfully for them it was not raining. It was still very wet so they still got spayed by the passing cars but not nearly as much as before. This time they caught a ride right away and that had Sam thinking that he had a good chance of making it back on time to go to work. A tall, thin, pimply, faced young man in a small sports car was kind enough to pick them up. It was a tight fit but they both were able to get in. He took them within two blocks of Cheryl's sister-in-law's house. There they squeezed out of the small car and soon were at the house. Sam went in with Cheryl, but knew that he could not stay for long if he was going to make it back on time. It was only ten o'clock when they arrived, but Sam knew he could have a hard time finding a ride back. Jackie answered the door and let them into the front room where her two boys were watching television. Jackie looked at them after they were inside and said, "How did you get all wet?" Cheryl answered her, "You will never believe how we got here. We hitchhiked all the way from Crescent." Looking amazed Jackie said, "At this time of night? You've got to be kidding. Why did you hitchhike? Did Sam's car break down?"

"Yes, I was going to hitchhike up here by myself but Sam wouldn't let me."

"You did the right thing Sam." Jackie said, while holding her arms around her boys who were standing and leaning against her as she spoke. Sam then said, smiling, "Yes, it was all her idea." Then his smile disappeared as he got serious and said, "I could not stop her and there was no way I was going to let her hitchhike up here on her own." Jackie looked at Cheryl and scolded, "Cheryl you shouldn't have hitchhiked up here, especially at night. It's too dangerous, haven't you heard all those stories about hitchhikers getting killed?" Cheryl sounding contrite said, "I know. I will never do it again mom, at least not in the pouring rain that's for sure."

"Sometimes Cheryl will do some crazy things." Jackie said, looking very serous as she turned to look at Sam. Then she turned quickly to Cheryl and said, "Don't you Cheryl?" Cheryl, feeling picked on, defending herself, "Sam don't believe a thing she says. Jackie! Are you trying to chase Sam away?" Cheryl said, as she looked at Jackie accusingly, then Jackie smiled and said, "Don't you think Sam should know the truth about you?" Cheryl was also smiling now as she answered, "No, I would not want him to know any of my dark secrets." The two boys filled with interest, looked back and forth at Cheryl and Jackie as they spoke. Sam could tell that Jackie and Cheryl were very good friends and Jackie with her brassy attitude reminded him even more of the singer Cher. He enjoyed the banter, but knew he must be on his way so he said, "Cheryl, I've got to go. I've got to catch the Crummy."

"You have to be at work in the morning?" Sandy said looking astonished. "Yeah at five-thirty in the morning."

"Cheryl you don't deserve this man." Sam looked at Cheryl, smiled and said. Yeah Cheryl remember that."

"I will Sam, you know that." Then Sam opened the door and said before he walked out. I've really got to go. Bye everyone." He then kissed Cheryl while out on the porch, walked out onto the sidewalk and down the street.

As early as it was that night he was feeling confident about making it back to Crescent on time. There was very little traffic as he walked down the residential streets and onto the artery that led towards the river. He knew there was not much of a chance of getting a ride to Crescent until he got down to the interstate, so he hurried down the street trying to get to the highway as quick as he could. It turned out to be a much longer walk than he had thought. A lot of his precious time was being wasted walking along that empty street that had many large boarded up buildings the closer he got to the river. He did not see a soul in all of his walking from Jackie's house and he was glad that was the case. He'd heard of all the crime they had, in big cities like Portland, in neighborhoods like he was walking through as he got closer to the river. Television news shows, and drama's, were full of the stories. His thoughts quickened his already fast pace. He finally got to one of the many bridges that crossed the Willamette River. It was one of the older bridges, one with a great metal frame of huge steel beams that arched high above Sam as he walked quickly across the bridge.

One thing, though, it had not rained since he left Cheryl at her sister-in-laws house, which was something for him to be thankful for. As he approach the other end of the bridge and had crossed over the river, he could see a road running underneath the bridge. Spanning across and above that road was a large green sign. It had written on it what Sam was looking for, Interstate Five South. Knowing that Interstate Five was so close made him feel lucky again, but there was a problem. The bridge still reached a long way into the city before it ended on the other side. So if he walked to the end of the bridge it would take him too much time to get back to the highway underneath him. He looked for a way down to the road below him and true to his better luck there was a stairway down to it. He could not believe it but there it was so he started climbing down the stairway. The road was not interstate Five; it was an entrance ramp to the highway, which to him was just as good. When he got down to the bottom of the stairway, and to the road he was standing on a sharp curve of the ramp just as it came out of a tunnel that ran under that end of the bridge. The cars that came out of the dark tunnel opening were going slow enough to get a good look at Sam, and the road had two lanes with plenty of room on the side for them to stop away from traffic. The problem was the drivers would have to make up their minds in a hurry or they would be around the sharp corner and gone. Looking at it caused Sam's hope to wane, and that's when it started raining. His mood was quickly souring as he stared up at the rain coming down in the lights and shadows of the concrete and metal wasteland. Such a lonely place, he thought, looking so alien to human life even the life that whizzed by Sam in their warm, dry cars. Sam stood there very tired from his long walk, and his long tough day, and getting wetter by the minute. He could have walked on further trying to find a better place, to catch a ride, but he didn't want to take another step. So soaked and miserable from the cold he wrapped his arms around himself for a little heat, but still reached out and stuck his thumb up whenever a car came by, and told himself that if he had to he would stay right there till it got daylight he wasn't moving an inch.

After a few cars passed without stopping, an old beat up, dark green panel truck came out of the tunnel traveling much slower than the cars before it. He was thinking of not putting his thumb out when the old truck approached. As cold and miserable as he was, though, he put his thumb out to see if the truck would stop. The truck did stop for him so he slowly jogged over to it. A little leery. He needn't have worried, because sitting in the front seat was a small thin young man in his mid-twenties wearing long hair down to his shoulders tied up on both sides of his head Indian style, and wearing a goatee, bib overalls, and a blue work shirt. Sitting close beside him was a girl who looked like she had to be in her middle teens. Sam thought she was pretty with her long blond hair, big blue eyes and wearing a hippie slave shirt. The first thought Sam had, after looking in the window, was that they had to be a hippie and his girl friend. All he ever heard of them is that they believed in was peace and love. They were going to Salem. So Sam got in. It would not get him far, but he would be out of the rain for a while, and to a better place to catch a ride. After he got in back and they started to drive off, the girl in the front seat turned around and, smiling, said in a friendly manner, "What's your name?"

"My name is Sam Jackson."

"My name is Linda and this is Mike here beside me."

"Hi, I'm sure glad that you stopped and picked me up. I was afraid no one was going to pick me up and I was getting very wet." Mike said without looking around, "I always stop for hitchhikers because I've hitched rides myself and know how hard it is sometimes."

"Well, I sure am happy that you stopped for me." Sam wanting to be friendly because they had stopped for him, but finding it hard to think of something finally said, "Mike, you must be a carpenter. You have all these carpentry tools back here?"

"Yes, I do a little carpentry work for people sometimes. We have a small farm where we raise vegetables, herbs. And a few goats. We sold some of our herbs today at a little Farmers Market. Then we visited some friends before we decided to drive back to Salem where we have our farm. You were lucky. We come to Portland every week on this day, but usually are home long before now."

"Yes, I do feel lucky. I know people don't like to pick up hitchhikers at night." Sam was thinking that Mike didn't like him much thinking he probably sensed he wasn't sympathetic to the hippie philosophy. Although there were some things about them that he admired, peace and Love were great things, but he thought hardly practical in the world that he knew and lived in. The pretty young girl looked over the seat and said, "How come you were hitchhiking so late at night?"

"I was in Crescent today. That's a little town south of Eugene. My girlfriend wanted to get to Portland badly so she was going to hitchhike up here by herself. I have a car but it's broken down. I didn't want her to hitchhike up here by herself, especially at night, so I came with her. Now I have to hitchhike back because I have to go to work this morning. I work in the woods setting chokers. I have to be in Crescent at five thirty. Do you know what time it is?" The girl then looked at Mike and said, "Mike what time is it?"

"It's almost three o'clock. I think you'll have a hard time making it to Crescent by five thirty." Sam who knew he was right said," Yeah, it sure looks that way." It wasn't long after they picked up Sam that they were turning off at the Salem exit where Sam got off to try his luck again. Sam did not have to wait long before he got a ride in a fancy red sports car. It was just for another short run to Albany but he was making progress. Then he got the ride he was looking for all the way to Crescent. On his way to Crescent the sky started brightening in the East as the sun started coming up. It was bad news for Sam for he knew for sure then that it was too late for him to catch the Crummy to get to work. When Sam got home, he was so very worn out and tired that he went right to bed and slept long and hard. He slept all day Friday waking for short time to eat in the evening, and then going right back to bed to sleep until Saturday morning. Sam waited until Sunday afternoon to call Cheryl. He was feeling a little worried about whether or not Cheryl really cared about him as much as he cared about her. Cheryl had been so insistent on getting to Portland just to help her sister move, even willing to hitchhike a night in the rain to do it, that it worried him. He was feeling very alone and down when he called and heard her. "Hello."

"Cheryl, this is Sam. I just thought that I would give you a call and see how you're doing?"

"I'm doing all right. How are you Sam?"

"I'm kinda lonely without you."

"I miss you to Sam."

"Cheryl can I come and get you. I got my car running again. I really miss you." Then it came what Sam expected and dreaded. "Sam, I'm going to stay up here for awhile at Jackie's. I think that you should think about whether or not you should leave your wife or not." A sinking feeling suddenly took hold of Sam. The feeling he got every time he thought he was going lose her. He felt this was coming and now it was here. Feeling helpless, like there was nothing he could do about it. He said weakly just to be saying something. "You don't want to come and live with me here in Crescent?" He was feeling so down knowing for sure Cheryl was leaving him because he felt she would not change her mind, once it was made up. She was that kind of person. He thought there would be no changing her mind, but he had to try, as Cheryl said, "Sam, do you really want to leave your wife and child?"

"Cheryl you really don't want to come to Crescent?"

"No, Sam, You can come up to see me, but I don't want to live down there with you. At least not right now anyway." That made him feel a little better knowing that there still was a chance she would move in with him. "I left my wife and child for you. I left them for you. I cannot change what I have done. She won't take me back now."

""Sam, I will stay up here for a couple of weeks and see how I feel and you can decide what you want."

"Cheryl, I know what I want and that is you."

"I know Sam and I love you, but let's give it some time." She was not going to come to Crescent, he knew it, and there was nothing he could say to change her mind. The more he talked to her the worse he felt so upset he abruptly said, "Okay, I'll call you sometime this week since that is all I can do. "Goodbye, Cheryl."

"Goodbye, Sam'" Sam was feeling so bad that he went right to bed even though it was only six o'clock in the afternoon. He had lost his wife and now he truly felt that he would surely lose Cheryl.

CHAPTER ELEVEN
CHERYL'S ORDEAL

Sam was feeling so upset that he waited until the next Saturday to call Cheryl. When he called her, just as he had thought, she had not changed her mind about coming to live with him. He had been paid and could have driven to see her, if she would have let him, and he thought she would have, but being upset like he was, he thought that if she did not want to come and live with him, he would just see how she felt not seeing him for awhile. Being by himself, though, it was very lonely and getting lonelier. It was not easy for him to stay home that weekend and not run to her, but he held firm. During the week he had gone to see his folks a few times. Otherwise he just stayed home and lived with his loneliness. Brenda sent him a letter that week telling him that her folks had gotten her a lawyer, and that she was going to file for divorce. She also told him that the lawyer had told her that he would have to pay her child support. He knew it was his duty to support his son, and he would, but he wanted to see Patrick as often as he could no matter where he lived. He didn't care if he had to travel all the way to New Mexico, or to china, or the moon he would see him and be a part of his life. At the very end of her letter Brenda wrote that she still loved him very much and wanted him to come back to her. Sam had still not forgotten the night that she tore at his heart as she cried for so long in his arms. The night he was ready to go back to her. He still wanted to give his life with

Cheryl a chance, though, that is if she would give him a chance, and that was something he did not know. He had taken the drastic step of telling Brenda that he wanted to leave her and now that she was gone he felt he needed to give Cheryl and him a good chance, because of his love for her. He had left Brenda out of that great love for Cheryl, but she seemed to be slipping away from him, and that worried him very much during his lonely nights. By Wednesday night a very lonely Sam, without Brenda or Cheryl, wrote Brenda back and told her that he still loved her and missed her and Patrick. In his empty, quiet, and so lonely, apartment he felt so close to her, as he wrote that letter, that he thought he would just go ahead and write her that he would come back to her, but he didn't. As he had gotten lonelier that week it had gotten so easy for him to feel that Cheryl would never come to live with him. So although he did not tell Brenda in that letter he was coming back to her. He knew he would tell her, maybe he thought, in his next letter. He knew that after that long night that she had cried on his shoulder he had been ready to go back to her, and he knew he was still ready to do that.

The next night Sam had only eaten a sandwich for supper and gone to bed early. Later that night he was roused abruptly from a deep sleep by a loud booming. A rare thunderstorm for Crescent had blown in, and it was a huge one, a heavy wind was blowing the limbs of a tree so that the limbs were continually hitting and scrapping against his bedroom window. That racket along with the continuing booming of the thunderstorm and the heavy rain blowing against his window kept him awake. He thought as he lay there that the thunderstorm must be one of the hardest to ever hit the area. He couldn't remember one being any worse in all the time that he had grown up in Crescent. He had seen lots and lots of rain storms because in Oregon there was constant rain in the winter, but very few really bad thunderstorm with the lighting and all the wind like the one that was going through then. It finally died down enough, after almost an hour, that he was able to go to sleep but at around one o'clock in the morning he was waken again, this time by a knocking sound. He knew no one would be knocking on his door at that time of night so he just started to go back to sleep. Then he thought he heard someone open the door. In the quiet of the night he could hear all the way across his little apartment to the front door. He knew he had locked the front door it was something he never forgot to do it. Then he heard the heavy steps of someone walking down the hall. It was a sound that he was very familiar with. He knew it was Cheryl because she still had his key and she took heavy steps because she walked different than anyone he had ever known. She walked with long, stiff legged, strides, making her steps heavy and she swaying a little with each step while always landing on her heels. Then a very cold and very wet Cheryl landed on his back and woke Sam like an electric shock. She put her hand over his mouth, a hand that was a cold as ice and said to him, "Be Quiet. Don't say a thing, don't move." She was not only cold, in her soaked cloths, but also very taut and tense as she held him tightly. Sam wondered what could be wrong as they lay there still as stones. He could only think that someone was after her, and that she was very afraid of whoever it was. It wasn't long before she whispered in his ear. "Burr, I'm cold." Sam whispering back to her said, "Yea, I can tell that you're very cold. You need to get out of those wet cloths and get under the covers." Quickly she slid off Sam's back and pulled her cloths off. She then got back in bed where Sam put his arms around her and pulled her ice cold, and very tense nude body up close to him. She felt like a big icicle in his arms. He had to force himself to hold her she was so cold. Sam was so very cold but knew he was getting Cheryl warm, whispered, "What's the matter, is someone after you?

"Sam, you won't believe what happened to me tonight." Just then Sam again heard the knocking on his door. "Cheryl quickly whispered very softly, "Don't say a word. It's the cab driver that brought me here."

"You took a cab all the way from Portland?" Sam whispered incredulously."

"No, he brought me from Eugene." Cheryl said as quietly as she could. "I told him I didn't have any money, but I knew someone here in Crescent who would pay for the ride if he brought me here. I know you don't get paid until Friday, and wouldn't have any money, so I had him park out on sixth street and then I walked to your door. I'm sure glad I kept your key. He watched me walk to your door, but there are so many doors I don't think he really knows which one I entered." Just then the knocking stopped causing them to stop talking and to try to be as quiet as they could in the little apartment. After they were quiet for awhile Sam said, "Your right I don't have any money, but I got paid last week. I bought some groceries, paid some bills, and paid my folks some money I owed them. I could have driven to Portland last week, but I've owed my folks for a long time, and you're here anyway."

"Oh, I thought it was this coming Friday that you got paid." Sam thought about going to the door and telling the driver he had no money but would mail it to him, or he could come and get it when he had the money. He knew though that the cab driver might call the police and have Cheryl arrested when he found out he couldn't pay So Sam and Cheryl continued to hold each other tightly in the very quiet room as Cheryl slowly warmed up causing Sam to enjoy holding her so much more. Staring at each other with there faces inches apart Sam said, "How did you get to Eugene?"

"Sam, it all started tonight at the bar where my brother hangs out every night. He invited me to have some drinks and play some pool. I drank way too much and was pretty drunk when I started missing you. I decided I was going to find someway to get to Crescent no matter what to be with you, and no one was going to stop me. I couldn't get anyone to bring me not my brother, no one. I finally was able to talk this young kid, Jerry, into bringing me. He is kind of slow and a good friend of my brother. I know my brother is going to kill me when he finds out what happened. I told Jerry I would go out with him if he brought me here. I know I shouldn't have lied to him, but I just wanted to see you so badly. Jerry just bought him a new thunderbird. It's really a beautiful car. Coming down here he was going to fast in that heavy rain though, and skidded off the road and hit a guardrail, and it beat up his car pretty bad. Both of us were alright though. It was nice that a lot of cars stopped, to see how we were, as we were standing there under an underpass, out of that heavy rain, waiting for the police to arrive. It was really pouring down then, when one of the guys that stopped started talking to me. I told him I was going to Crescent and he offered to take me. So I left Jerry there. See what I do for you. You know I'm just a fool for love, and my brother is going to hate me.

Sam lay there and began thinking that he had been very wrong in thinking that she didn't love him, and was going to leave him as he continued to listen quietly to her wild story about all she had gone through just to see him, and then she told him the worst part of her trip to she him. "The guy that gave me the ride kept trying to grab me; I had to fight him off. He stopped along the highway by that Denny's just this side of Eugene, that is when I really got scared, and then when he tried to grab me again I fought him off and jumped out of the car and I ran to the restaurant, and didn't come out for a long time. I was so scared of that guy." As Cheryl spoke about her experience and Sam visualized the things that she had gone through, especially with the guy who gave her the ride, and obviously tried to rape her, his anger built and he yelled loudly, "What an Asshole." Cheryl quickly shushed him. He had forgotten he was supposed to be quiet. He just felt so very sorry for her and for what she had gone through in the middle of a huge thunder storm to see him. He pulled her closer to him as she continued to talk. "I bought a cup of coffee and waited a long time before I went outside. I was so scared of that guy. I called the police and the policeman that came was nice, and took my information, but with not much to go on he said they would probably not be able to catch him. After he left I finally went outside to try to catch a ride. Lightening was flashing and the rain was pouring down so hard that my cloths were soaked before I left the restaurant's parking lot. I couldn't stand it out there. I was so wet. I gave up right away and came back to the restaurant. I don't think I've ever seen it rain so hard my life. Sam broke in and said, "Yes I heard the thunder and thought a tree was going to break my bedroom window because its limbs were hitting it so hard."

"You had that storm down here to?"

"Yes and I can't believe you were out in that storm, and here I was in this warm bed."

"You see what I do for love."

"Yes, Cheryl I see what you do for love." He really did believe she loved him after all that she had gone through that night to see him. Although just earlier that night he had not believed she loved him, and wanted to live with him. Then Cheryl continued her story as she said, "When I called the taxi. At first the driver didn't want to take me, but as wet as I was I think he felt sorry for me. He is really a nice guy and I hate that I cannot pay him." They heard the loud knocking on the door again causing them to stop whispering and to lie still as they continued to hold each other. This time the knocking lasted a long time. One of Sam's neighbors opened his door and yelled at the taxi driver to knock it off so he could get some sleep. Then the knocking stopped for good. Sam had gotten cold holding Cheryl and warming her, so he got more blankets and then they warmed themselves more with joyful sex. They were back together again and Sam knew that after what his crazy wonderful Cheryl had gone through she must really want to live with him, and marry him.

Chapter Twelve
Living With Cheryl

The next evening, after Sam gotten off work, Cheryl had his supper ready. She had put together a meal from the groceries that he had bought which were mostly precooked and food that was easy to prepare. Sam was no cook. He had planned to go to a University of Oregon football game that weekend. He was going to ask his brother to go with him, but that was before Cheryl showed up. Since she was with him now, he asked her if she wanted to go to the game and she was willing. He had money because Stud had finally paid him the fifty dollars that he had loaned him.

That Saturday they drove to Eugene to see the game at Autzen Stadium. It was a big game for the Oregon Ducks. They were having a good season, but were not favored to beat the Southern California Trojans. The team that often dominated the Pac Ten football Conference.

The Trojans almost always beat the ducks, but this season Sam thought the Ducks had a chance for an upset and he wanted to be there to cheer them on. On their trip to Eugene to the game, it started raining. They were not happy about that because Sam had no umbrella. There was no place on their way that was close so that he could buy one either, and there was not enough time, before the game started, for Sam to go very far out of his way to get one. They had just enough time to get to the game for the opening kick off. Sam was able to stop and run into a small store and buy a sheet of plastic to cover them though. As they drove on to the Stadium it was still lightly raining. Sam drove slowly into the large parking area that surrounds Autzen Stadium following a long line of cars. As they crept along behind the cars Sam said, I never asked you if you like football. I guess it is kind of late to be asking but do you?"

"Yes Sam, I like football."

"Do you ever watch it on television?"

"I don't usually, but sometimes when I'm with my brothers or when Mike, Jackie's husband, is watching a game. He really likes football."

"Good, I know you'll like this game. It's sure to be a good one." After the car quieted for awhile as they waited, Cheryl volunteered, "My father was a football coach." Surprised, Sam said, "Where did he coach?"

"Klamath Falls."

"Did he coach the high school team?"

"Yes, he was an assistant coach at Klamath Falls High School. We lived there for a long time." Her answer caused Sam, as they still sat there waiting in line with the other cars, to began thinking of Cheryl as a high school student. It amused him, to think of her that way as a high school student of her being like the girls he had gone to school with. Which one of the many girls in his school would she have been like? What crowd would she have ran with? He even wondered if, back then, she would have liked him or would he have liked her. He pictured her walking the halls of his old high school with all the immature fools like him. Who would she have stopped to talk to? Who would she have ignored? Would she have been one of the kids who were mature and ready for the real world in high school? He did not think that would have been her, and he knew if it was she would have ignored him for sure. The more he thought about it the more that he could not see her being in the high school he went to, they were both older now, but she just didn't seem to fit in his small town school, but that was one of the things that attracted him to her. Cheryl broke into his thoughts as they crept along behind the long line, as she said speaking seriously in a low voice while starting ahead, "It was while we were in Klamath Falls that he started having his problems." Sam suddenly alert and very curious, said, "What kind of problems did he have?"

"That is when he first started having to go to the county hospital." Sam felling sympathy for her said,

"What was wrong with him? Was he sick?"

"In a way. The county hospital is a Psychiatric Hospital." Cheryl continued to speak softly and not look at Sam. She just sat there very still beside him staring at the car in front of them. A little shocked Sam didn't know what to say. As he looked at her so quiet beside him he knew she must be lost in some unhappy memories of her father. He would have liked to have asked her about those memories, but did not say a word before she started talking again. "Although we liked it there, Things got pretty bad for us in Klamath Falls especially when my father lost his job and we had little money. Then he had to go to the hospital for good so my mother moved back to Portland, with us kids, so she could be near her family. I wished we could have stayed in Klamath Falls. I liked it much better than Portland. I have never like Portland. " This was the first time Cheryl had mentioned her father and now he understood why. Sam knew that her mother lived alone but he had never asked about her father guessing that she did not want to talk about him. He did feel he was slowly learning the reasons for the sadness that he always felt he saw in her though. He was glad that she felt like sharing this big and sad part of her life with him. Cheryl quieted then and continued to stare ahead as they waited. Sam sensing that she did not want to say more about her father, or talk at all said nothing to her.

Sam finally was directed to a parking spot, by the parking attendants, and quickly parked his car. The sun was shining brightly as it peeked though openings in the clouds, and it was only lightly sprinkling as they rushed to the ticket booth to buy their tickets. Sam could feel the excitement of the crowd as he and Cheryl walked up the big ramp that was choked with people and into the stadium. It was the same excitement that held him tightly. He had bought two of the cheaper seats so that meant that they sat far up in the Stadium in an end zone seat, but he didn't care. He was going to see the game. He was where he loved to be, at an Oregon football game. They hurried to their seats and got there just in time to see the opening kick off. It was very cold and very wet, but the sun was warming them a little as it sneaked out between the clouds. Sam brought a blanket that he always carried in his car and laid it down on the very wet concrete seat. Even thought the sun was warming them a little Cheryl had her arms wrapped tightly around herself and was shivering as she sat beside Sam on the blanket that was already soaked half way through. Sam could tell she was feeling miserable but the cold did not bother him at all as he could not imagine it ever being so bad that he would not stay and watch an Oregon football game. He quickly unraveled the plastic sheet he had just bought and pulled it over their heads because it was starting to mist a little, and they then pulled the sides of the white plastic sheet tightly around their heads so they could watch the game.

The game started out good for the ducks as they recovered a fumble right away causing the crowd to fill the stadium with a tremendous roar. They recovered the ball on the Trojans twenty-five yard line and quickly scored a touchdown, which was accompanied by an even louder roar than the first one, and a roar that lasted twice as long. The crowd was really into the game early as everyone in the stadium was yelling including Sam and Cheryl. Everyone, that is, except the few Trojan supporters in the stadium. That was about all the offensive action in the first half, though; because of the good defensive play of both teams and the wet field. It had darkened overhead and started raining hard in the middle of the first quarter which made it harder for the offensive players to play and the crowd to watch the game. Sam and Cheryl huddled tightly together beneath the plastic sheet trying to stay warm and dry as they could. During the third quarter, the huge Southern Cal offensive line had started to wear down the much smaller Oregon defensive line. They opened big holes for their backs on a drive that reached the Oregon end zone to tie the game. They later in the third quarter tacked on a field goal to go ahead by three points. That is the way the score lasted through the middle of the forth quarter. Late in that quarter, though, in a steady downpour, and to the surprise of almost everyone in the stadium, Oregon had slowly cobbled together a drive that had pushed the ball to a first down on the Trojans thirty-eight yard line. After three downs they had moved the ball nowhere just like they had done for most of the game. The ball still stood there on the thirty-eight yard line. Sam, and everyone in the stadium knew that Oregon would never have another chance to win the game, so they had to go for it on forth down and they did. After a timeout, the crowd full of anticipation filled the stadium with noise as the Oregon team broke the huddle. Sam yelling as loud as anyone, very glad that they were driving for the end zone where he and Cheryl were sitting. They had one of the best seats in the house for that final play.

Sam was thinking how lucky could he get, and how all those people in the expensive seats under the roof on the fifty yard had to be wishing they were sitting where he was sitting.

Dan Fouts, the Oregon quarterback, took the snap and faded back from the center. Sam could see the play developing as Oregon's best receiver split out to the left side of the field was streaking for the goal post, but once in the middle of the field, he cut sharply towards the flag on his left and the one that was right in front of Sam. The receiver was running straight towards Sam and Cheryl, with the defensive back tightly on him, not giving him an inch. The play was long developing, but the Oregon line, knowing what was at stake, held their men at bay keeping them away from Fouts. Then Fouts eyeing his man reached down deep inside him and with the adrenaline surging in his veins, he heaved the ball as high and as far as he could. That is when Sam and Cheryl, and the rest of the crowd around them, rose slowly to their feet as they followed the ball as it first soared high into the air, and by the time it reached it highest point they were all up and standing. They all stood there in quiet anticipation not a sound was heard as Sam and all the fans around him stood with their heads arched upwards. They all were like someone in the eye of a tornado waiting for the storm to start again. The ball zoomed down towards the flag; the receiver had seen the ball and was running desperately towards the flag with the defensive back still inches away from him. He gathered himself as he neared the flag and then launched himself into the air diving towards the flag, and while lying flat out in the air he reached the ball with his finger tips. Then he landed flat on the wet turf sliding over the flag with the ball still clutched in his hands and the roar of the crowd in his ears, scoring a touchdown and winning the game for Oregon. The crowd erupted like a volcano with Sam and Cheryl yelling as loud as anyone in the crowd. The thunder continued through the successful extra point kick and even after the teams had lined up for the Oregon kick off. The crowd spurred on by the many years of losing to the mighty Trojans.

Oregon, buoyed by the touchdown, hung on to win the game. Sam thought that touchdown play was the best pass play he had ever seen, and it was Oregon who had scored the great touchdown and he had seen it live. It could not have been any better for him. He and Cheryl had a wonderful ride home, after the game, both of them in great spirits especially Sam. He felt as good as if he had played in the game himself.

The following weekend Cheryl wanted to go to Portland to pick up the cloths that she had left at Jackie's. So the next Saturday they were on their way to Portland. This time not hitchhiking but riding comfortably in Sam's car along that long, mostly very straight, highway that runs from Crescent to Portland through the wide and flat Willamette Valley. The Coast Range of Mountains was far away across the flat valley bottom to their left, and the much higher Cascade Mountains, with their three sisters clustered together were closer, and to their right as they drove steadily north on Interstate Five. It was one of those beautiful winter days in Oregon, that doesn't come around often enough, when the sun comes out after stormy weeks like a blessing from God. When the air is so clear and colors so bright it makes one glad they are alive, just to experience it. They drove serenely down the highway feeling so good on that beautiful morning, enjoying the scenery and each other. Sam sat with his arm around Cheryl for miles, quietly enjoying the ride as they rolled down the road. They no longer needed to talk to enjoy each other's company, but as they neared Portland, Cheryl said, "Sam after we pick up my cloths could you take me to see someone? It won't take long."

"Sure I'll take you anywhere. We can stay up here all day if you want."

"No, I'm not going to stay long. I'm just going to run in and run out. I'm going to pick up some whites."

"Alright." Sam had been using the little white pills every day for the last week. Cheryl had brought some in a bag with her the night she woke him on that very stormy night, but they had already used all of them. After a long but comfortable ride, they arrived in Portland, and then visited with Jackie, and her family while picking up Cheryl's clothes. After they left Sam made the little side trip that Cheryl wanted him to make.

Cheryl had Sam drive through a neighborhood that was close to Jackie's house, but the neighborhood was very different. The houses were much older and smaller, and some were very run down. A few of them had old, worn out, cars sitting on blocks in front of them. As Sam drove through the neighborhood, he began feeling a little uneasy knowing that they could be arrested for what they were going to do. He had never really worried about carrying the pills around before. Always rationalizing that they shouldn't really be illegal, like Cheryl had told him, and he had never heard of anyone getting arrested for using the pills either. He just never heard anything about them. Marijuana and heroin yes, but never amphetamines. To Sam, though, what they were going to do now was different. They or Cheryl was going to be buying pills from a dealer. He sure was not going to tell Cheryl that he was nervous about it, though. If she was not worried, he certainly was going to try not to be. They drove to the edge of the residential area and parked by a big, dried out, grassy field edged by a grove of trees and brush. The field was on one side of them and a line of houses was on the other. Cheryl got out walked between two of the old houses, dodging an old jalopy, and over to the next block where she turned right when she reached the sidewalk and walked out of Sam's sight. Sam looked around nervously to check out the cars that were parked on the street. He started thinking that he was acting like the drug addicts he had seen in the movies watching for the police, which was exactly what he was doing. He also wondered what kind of people Cheryl was dealing with. Would they hurt her if they got suspicious of her?" Then he wondered if he had been watching too many movies about drugs. He was very relieved when she got back safely with her little plastic bag of pills. After they were out on the road and driving back to Crescent, Sam worries, about having the drugs quickly eased and then disappeared.

CHAPTER THIRTEEN
LOGGING IN THE SNOW

It was late January and Sam and Cheryl had been living together for over a month. It had been a very cold month and there was a lot of snow covering the tops of the Cascade Mountains. High in those mountains is where Boney Roberts and his little crew were logging.

One morning when Sam and the crew were riding in the Crummy on their way to work, and were nearing their logging site in the mountains, they noticed a little snow on the ground and as they climbed closer to where they were logging, it got steadily deeper. Soon the scene was completely white. Snow was thick on the ground and stacked on the brush and trees, and when they got up to the logging site they found the ground covered with more than two feet of snow. They would not have made it up that far up the mountain, in that deep snow, if someone had not been there ahead of them, and plowed the snow off the gravel road for them. Sam had worked in a little snow already, but two feet of snow was more than he ever dreamed he would have to work in. Palmer parked the Crummy on the bottom of the unit before the road wound its way up and around the mountain to the landing where the Yarder and Loader were parked. From way below Sam could just see top of the Yarder's Tower. They were on the very edge of where the big lines reached out to pick up logs, and where the blocks were hooked on stumps. Sam felt lucky, in one way, they usually had to walk down though the brush to get where they logged this time they simply had to get out of the old Crummy, and walk about twenty yards to be where they were to start logging. They had stopped where they found Boney's pickup with him standing there looking up and surveying the snow covered mountainside. Sam was staring out the window at all the snow when they stopped beside Boney. He was sure that Boney would not have them work that day. He just knew he would never make them get out there and freeze in that cold snow, as deep as it was. He knew how cold working in two or three inches of ice cold, slushy, snow could be, but this snow was much deeper. He had his rubber coat and pants to wear, but knew they would not keep him dry for long, they never did. They would not keep him dry when he was just working in the rain. As soon as they stopped Palmer and Stud put on their boots, and rubber coats and pants, and then got of the truck and started pushing their way through the snow. Sam didn't say a word but could not believe that they were going to work in that deep snow. He knew they would have to walk through the cold, snow covered, brush getting soaking wet as they did, and also have to trudge through accumulated snow above their knees. He had been freezing cold in the icy rain before, and knew this deep snow would make him colder than that. Sam waited to put on his boots because he did not want to get out of that warm truck. He did not want to lose his job either, so he quickly laced up his boots and jumped out into the snow. He started pushing himself through the snow trying to catch up with Palmer who was already climbing through the snow caked bush to where they were going to start logging. Sam had to walk right by Boney who was now sitting in his warm truck. Sam, looking and feeling miserable, hoped Boney would tell him that everyone was going home, but he said nothing as Sam trudged pass him. Sam should have known better because he knew that if there was any way to log at all, Boney was going to log. As he walked through the snow he found it was easier than he thought it would be, because the snow was so dry and powdery. It was not like the snow he had worked in before, and the kind they got in Crescent. In Crescent the snow was wetter and would quickly turn into a watery slush. Since the snow was so dry and powdery it did not get him nearly as wet as he thought. It did not melt. In fact in his warm cloths and rubber pants and coat, he was soon sweating as he hurriedly followed Palmer and Stud through the snow covered brush. Brush, which would have soaked him if the snow had not been so dry. When he got to where the logs were, he had to slow down because he could not tell where the logs were beneath the snow unless they were very big ones. When Sam got the where the other two choker setters were, they had a fire going and were standing there very warm and cozy by the fire, waiting for the Yarder to start and send the chokers down to them. Palmer had carried a can of diesel into the brush, which made it very easy for him to start a fire and keep it going in the snow. Standing by the warm fire, Sam was feeling a lot better thinking that working in the snow was not going to be so bad after all. They did not have to go to work right away, either, allowing them to stay by the warm fire longer. Boney had to plow the road up to the landing with the Caterpillar, so the Crummy and the logging trucks would be able to get up to the landing high above them. The chokers finally did make it out into the brush, though, and then they sent the first turn of logs out from the very back of the skid row. That way the first turn would scrape some of the snow off the logs above them so it would be easier to find the logs and put chokers on them. Pulling the logs in created a lot of icy mud which was worse than the snow, especially when Sam had to get down on his knees, in the deep mud, to dig a hole under a log for a choker. The logging was a little slower because the snow made things very slippery, especially when they were walking on the top of the logs even though they had spiked cork boots on. The snow would clog up the spikes keeping from biting in, and they also had to watch carefully when they were stepping in the deep snow because they never knew what was underneath. There was definitely no running on the logs like Sam would always do when there was no deep snow. They got out quite a few logs though, and sent almost the usual amount of loaded trucks down the hill that day, surprising Sam and they knew pleasing Boney.

At home that evening Sam, as soon as he walked in the door almost yelled at Cheryl, "You would not believe how much snow I was working in today! We were working in over two feet of snow and more than that in the drifts. It reached above my knees almost to my waist in the drifts.

"Sam! You didn't work in that much snow. You're lying. They wouldn't make you work in that much snow."

"Boney sure did. Boney would log in a tornado. It was so deep we couldn't tell where the logs were until we pulled a couple of turns over them and scraped the snow off."

"You must have been freezing out there."

"It wasn't as bad as I thought. The snow was powdery and dry."

"I still don't see how they could make you work in that much snow and work in it all day."

"This morning when I saw all that snow, and then knew I was going to have to work in it, I was ready to quit, but there is no way I could do that." Cheryl looked at Sam, smiled and said, "I'll make you forget about being so cold. This wild woman will get you warm tonight." Sam laughed before saying, "I can't wait."

"Well you're going to have to take a shower first." Looking disappointed Sam said. "Okay but do I have to?" Cheryl then scolded, "Yes, you have to."

"All right, but I'll make it a fast one." He hurried off to take his shower to wash all the mud off his body, and then his wild woman made him forget about his cold day in the woods.

Chapter Fourteen
New Rigging Slinger

A couple of weeks after the big snow Boney hired a new man to be the rigging slinger, pushing Stud out of the job that Sam was doing anyway. Jerry Smart was the kid's name. Sam had been working for Boney for more than nine months, but Boney or Palmer hadn't made him Rigging Slinger because, he thought, they didn't think he had enough experience. Jerry had worked in the woods for five years and had been a rigging slinger before, and had even worked as a logger in Alaska. Palmer became the hook, or hook tender, the name for the big boss in the brush. He would now just line up the new skid rows and carry the blocks, the big pulleys the cables ran through, and then hook them up to large stumps. He would now be like the hook tenders that worked for the big logging outfits. They would stay back at the blocks all the time, changing them. They, like him, had to be able to line up the blocks so the main line would be lined up so the chokers would be able to reach the most logs. He also had to know the best and fastest way for them to log a unit. A job Boney had done before, and of course he had to watch out for the safety of the crew. So the hook tender was paid mostly for their knowledge and experience, and always, like Palmer, they had been working in the woods for many years.

Jerry, the new rigging slinger, was four years younger than Sam, but Sam could tell right away that he knew what he was doing so he didn't mind. Jerry also liked drinking beer and would take his turn buying beer for the crew, which Sam definitely liked and he seemed to Sam to be an all right guy. He'd also let Sam set his own choker, which was just the way that he liked it. Jerry would signal with the whistle and help Stud set his choker like Palmer had done and leave the other one to Sam.

The rigging crew was sitting on a big log, on an unusual sunny winter day, just after they had sent a turn of logs in on the first day that Jerry started working, when Sam said to him, "Palmer told me you set chokers in Alaska. What was it like?" Jerry swung around on the log and looked at Sam and said, "It was dam good money but we would get snowed out in the winter. I never could get ahead. I couldn't make enough money in the summer to last me the whole year. "

"Did you live in a logging camp?"

"Yea, it was just like living in a small town. They had a company store, a post office, and just about anything else that you would want. They had the best food I have eaten in my life, but there wasn't a single woman in camp, and no place to go to get a drink. Now that was bad." As they kept talking the chokers came rattling back, interrupting Jerry as they were being dragged back through the brush by the Main line. Jerry stood up, when the chokers got close, and sent in one whistle followed quickly by three more. The chokers then stopped moving down hill and the big main line holding them started to rise from the ground, lifting the butt rigging where the chokers were hooked to the line, lifting the tangled chokers into the air. After the chokers were raised a little they heard a toot come from the landing. The sound Jerry made by squeezing his rubber handled whistle. They all ran towards the chokers and when they reached them, Sam and Stud each grabbed a dangling choker, which they pulled to two small but long logs. Logs that, new rigging slinger, Jerry had picked out for them while the last turn of logs, was being pulled into the landing. Sam jumped over his log, while Stud stepped on his on his way over it. They then pulled the nub end of their chokers over their logs and pushed that end of the stiff choker back under the logs to where the bell was in the middle of the choker. They quickly locked the nub into the bell with a snap setting their chokers, or noose around the logs, they then ran far enough out of the way to be safe from the logs and their long limbs when they started moving. Jerry squeezed his whistle once and the Main line started moving up the hill dragging the chokers with it. That caused the noose that had been created by the chokers being set around the logs, to tighten and to choke the logs. Then the logs jumped out of their nests and started crashing up the hill. The three choker setters watched the logs intently, until they thought they were safe. Then they sat down on their log seats again. Alaskan logging had always intrigued Sam. He had heard of guys going to Alaska, logging and living in the logging camps, while he was growing up. To go to Alaska and log the giant logs there and make thousands of dollars while doing it, which he had always heard was possible in only a summer's work, had always been a dream of his. His stepfather, who used to work in a lumber mill running a log barker, had worked in the woods when he was a young man. He had filled Sam's head with stories of logging, since he was a young boy, telling him stories of when they logged with Steam donkeys and Spar Trees, and when they had whistle punks and high climbers. He would often mention the old Steam Donkeys that were big steam engines, like the ones on the early trains. They called them steam pots and that is what they looked like, giant metal upside down pots. They would spew flumes of steam high into the air, from their big smoke stacks. They sat on two log sleds with a tin roof covering the engine and operator. Big round drums wound with steel cable were spun by the steam engine to reel in logs just like Boney's modern Yarder. The interesting thing to Sam was that instead of the tall steel pole they had on the modern Yarder to run the mainline up before running it down the hill into the brush, back then they would run the big line up a tall tree. That meant they had to have high climbers. The high climber would climb up the tall spar tree using only a strap that wrapped around him and the tree and big spurs or spikes tied to his boots. He would lean back against the strap and sink his spurs into the tree allowing him to walk up the tree as he swung the strap up the tree as he climbed. As he climbed he would cut the limbs off the tree with a hand saw that hung from a rope tied to his belt, and when he had climbed almost to the top of the tree he would take his saw and cut off the top of the tree. Once he topped the tree he would have to hang on tight as it swung violently back and forth, and then when it stopped swinging he would hang a block on it. Sam's stepfather had been a high climber so he had climbed and topped spar trees in the old days. He once told an unbelieving Sam that he was only paid fifty cents a day for being a high climber, and that he said was the highest paying job in the woods back then. His stepfather loved to tell the old stories. So Sam had grown up as a wide eyed young boy hearing about logging, and stories about loggers, and knowing many people in the small logging and lumber mill community who were loggers or lumber mill workers.

So Sam was curious and had to know more about logging in Alaska, on that warm day, so he asked Jerry, "On the weekends couldn't you go into the nearest town to party and have a good time?"

"No I didn't do that because they charged too much for the plane ride." Surprised Sam said, "You had to take a plane?"

Yea, we were logging on an island so everything had to be flown in and out. Most of the logging in Alaska is done on islands. The Island's are covered with trees."

"Was the ground steep?"

"It's about the same as here. Some of the logging is very steep though."

"Do they do any Cat logging?"

"I didn't see any where I was."

"I've always heard, since I was a kid, that you could make a lot of money logging in Alaska. I always wanted to give it a try."

"The money is good, but I tell you, Sam, I didn't think it was worth it." Sam did not want to hear that so he asked, "Why? I hear you can go up there for one or two seasons and make a big chunk of money. Like you say there is no way to spend your money so I would be able to save a bunch and put it in bank."

"Well, if you're good at saving money, but once the season was over I went through my money like a hot knife through butter. It might work if you could get a winter job here, but I always found that hard to do. Jobs in winter are hard to find around here."

"So it's not a good way to get a chunk of money for a new pickup and a down payment on a house?"

"It's been a couple of years since I worked in Alaska and I was pretty wild back then. I'm living with my girlfriend now and have settled way down. I would do a better job of keeping my money now, but I would still have to be able to get a winter job around here to do it."

The chokers came back, ending the conversation as they went back to work. Sam was disappointed that Jerry had dampened his Alaskan dreams. He knew though that he probably never would have followed through with them anyway. He continued to think that Jerry was going to be an all right guy though, because he knew what he was doing, was friendly enough, and did his share of the work. In fact, things were a little easier for everybody because Palmer would sometimes help with the chokers.

Chapter Fifteen
Sam Visits His Parents

As the weeks went on and Sam and Cheryl got used to living together, there were some evenings when Sam would leave Cheryl at the Apartment and walk over to his parent's house. It wasn't a long walk since they lived only three blocks from his apartment. He wouldn't take Cheryl because he knew his mother didn't like the fact that he was living with a woman who was not his wife, and Cheryl seemed to understand, at least at first. His Mother was very religious so she didn't want Sam to be living in sin. She also had not liked that he had left Brenda and his son, she really liked Brenda, and loved his son, but she didn't bother him about it on his visits so they were relaxed. He was still in love with Cheryl and was glad they were living together, but when he visited his folk's house he would read the letters Brenda would send him. That was when the last night that he had seen Brenda, when he had held her in his arms, and had rocked her for so long feeling the tears on his shoulder, would come back to him. The night that he found out how much she loved him and how he still loved her. At those times he would feel it was a mistake that he had left her.

Sam would sometimes stay long after he had read Brenda's letters, watching television with his mother and stepfather just as he had done so often when growing up. If felt so comfortable for him to be there with them, especially with all the turmoil his life had been going through.

As he sat in the living room warmed from the cold winter night by the big wood heating stove, he would feel so safe and secure just like when he was a little boy until his mom turned off the television as she and his stepfather retired for the night. Then he would trudge back to his apartment, in the cold, to crawl in beside a sleeping Cheryl and fall asleep.

At work things were going along very well. Sam was getting along with Jerry much better than he had got along with Palmer. Sam hardly ever saw Palmer anymore, which was alright with him. They were getting lots of logs out so everybody was happy, especially Boney, although he would never show it. The truck drivers who hauled the logs down the mountain to the huge Weyerhaeuser Lumber and Paper Mill were happy. They all owned their own trucks and were getting paid by the load and Boney's crew was sending them steadily down the road loaded.

Sam was getting along with Jerry so well that sometimes after work, before he went home to Cheryl, he would stop by a Tavern to play pool, and drink beer with him before going home. With his trips to his folks, and the evenings when he played pool, Sam was leaving Cheryl home alone two or three times a week. They were still having their wonderful lovemaking and enjoying each other's company when they were together, although Sam was finding out that Cheryl wasn't nearly as good a cook as Brenda was, but he doubted that many women were. One thing they were doing and that was using up Cheryl's little bag of white crosses very quickly. Sam really liked them and was taking more than he ever had before, taking one, and sometimes two, a day. They gave him energy when he was tired and seemed to make him more talkative. He always thought of himself as being a pretty quiet person, but when he took one of the little pills he had no trouble talking. He began to even think of himself as being more of a conversationalist when he wasn't taking them and maybe even a little smarter. Cheryl was very stingy with them though. If Sam wanted to take two at one time, or more than what she thought he should, she wouldn't let him have them. At those times when he wanted more she would sometimes tell him about the friend of hers who started taking more than one at a time. Her friend she told him started taking them, and as time went on he had to take more and more pills to get the same effect he was getting from one pill, and ended up getting hooked on them, and then not being able to sleep, and becoming violent and out of control at times, and having terrible withdrawals after taking them. Then he lost his job and started stealing to buy the pills and ended up in jail. The story always worked on Sam.

On one of his trips to his folk's house, his mother gave him another letter from Diana. This letter made him feel sad for she wrote about how badly she felt without him, and that she loved him and needed him. In the other letters she had just told him, only at the end of the letter, that she loved him, but in this letter she talked about her love for him all though the long letter. She told him much more about how she felt. The letter made him want so much to hold her and comfort her as memories of her and Patrick came flowing into his mind. He remembered how the winter before, when they had gotten an unusual heavy snow in Crescent. He and Patrick had played in the snow and built a big snowman, and how they had laughed when they made his face with a carrot and buttons. How he and Diana had laughed so loudly when looking at the snowman's face after he had lifted Patrick up to put one of his step dad's old floppy, worn out, work hats on the snowman's head.

He remembered how guilty he felt about keeping Patrick out in the snow so long because his hands got so cold that he started crying. He had lifted him up and ran to the warm apartment. There Brenda rubbed Patrick's hands, trying to warm them but they would not warm as he kept crying in pain. Finally, after what seemed like such a long time, and much to their relief the pain subsided and he stopped crying. Now Sam knew that when he was in pain he would never know it, and he would not be able to help him. Being so far away from him was weighing heavily on his mind.

The next visit after that visit his mother did not have a new letter from Brenda so he read her last one again and then knew he had to write her. He had written her before and told that he loved her, and had been ready to write her and tell her he was coming back to her, but did not because Cheryl had erased the fears he had of her not loving him and wanting to marry him when she, wet and half frozen, had landed on his back on the stormy night. He did write Brenda though, and tell her that he still loved her and missed her, and continued to write after that every week. Brenda would like clockwork answer every letter and tell him in each letter that she still loved him and wanted him to come back to her and Patrick.

With all of the time that Sam was spending away from the apartment Sam knew that Cheryl would eventually say something about it. He could tell as the weeks went by that she was unhappy about it, but it did not keep him from making his trips to read Brenda's letters, and the times he went out to drink beer and play pool with Jerry. Sam loved that Cheryl was smart and funny and the best friend a guy could have, but he also knew she could be tough. That was the way she was one time when he was getting ready to go to his folk's house. She said to him, "Sam you spend a lot of time visiting your folks and leaving me here all alone. I know that you said that you mother was very fond of Brenda, and did not want you to leave her, but if your going to marry me, she'll have to meet me sometime. I feel like a prisoner here. I never go any where except for my great adventures to the grocery store."

"Cheryl, I will have you meet my mother and step-father, but my mother just cannot get over the idea that I'm not still with Brenda. It will just take her a while, but she'll get used to the idea that I'm going to marry you. I know for sure that once we are married she will come around. His mother did want him to get back with Brenda and he knew with him writing her that she felt he would. He also knew that she would accept Cheryl even if he took Cheryl to see her that very night, and he knew that she would not even think of showing any unfriendliness to Cheryl. Sam, though, wanted to be able to continue to read Brenda's letter's and write her at his mother's house. He still felt he would marry Cheryl, but he wanted his connection to Brenda. He was letting himself slip into his same old dilemma. The same dilemma he was in before he told Brenda that he was leaving her, but he could not help himself he loved them both. Cheryl did get Sam to promise that he would see his folks less often, and to take her to see her sister-in-law the following weekend in Portland. Their trips to Portland were their dates and always a great times for both of them.

CHAPTER SIXTEEN
DOUBLE DATE

After a while Cheryl made a friend in Crescent although she was quite a bit younger than she was. Her new friend was Jerry's girlfriend, Cindy, who was living with him. She was from out-of-town like Cheryl and just as lonely. Jerry had asked Sam, after work if he and Cheryl wanted to go out with them to a drive-inn movie. Sam was a little surprised because he hadn't been out to drink and play pool with him in a long time. He found out, as he got to know Jerry better that he did not like him, but he told him that he'd ask Cheryl if she wanted to go, thinking that it would be good for Cheryl and him to get out. They made trips to Portland often, but seldom went out any where in Crescent, or Eugene and Springfield. Sam asked Cheryl that evening, and she quickly agreed to go.

Jerry came speeding into Sam's apartment's parking lot with his grey, primer coated Charger's, pipes roaring his arrival, he then quickly turned sharply into the parking place in front of Sam's apartment squealing his tires. It was a car sure to grab plenty of attention which was exactly what Jerry wanted from his rough looking car. Sam and Cheryl had been waiting for them, and since they were late they were watching for them through the picture window, at the front of the apartment, and saw the car squeal into the parking lot when it arrived. So they were soon out the door and into Jerry's hot car where introductions were made, and then they were off towards Eugene. The car was quiet, except for the low rumble of the pipes on Jerry's car, as they made their way quickly through Crescent. Sam had gotten to dislike Jerry ever since Palmer had got hurt and Jerry had taken over his job. They were still friends, but Sam felt he was letting his new job, as hook tender, go to his head. He started, Sam thought, to enjoy throwing his weight around way to much. He no longer was the happy, friendly, hard working kid that he was when he first started working for Boney. He now thought of himself as the big boss and was always very serious and acted, most of the time, like he was to good to even talk to Sam and Stud except to tell them what to do. Sam even thought he was trying to intimidate him, but Sam was not about to know tow to anyone, and he thought that Jerry might even be a little jealous of him because he was always working hard, and Boney liked that, and Jerry no longer worked hard or even tried. Sam never thought he would ever miss Palmer, but after a couple of weeks of Jerry as the hook tender, he did. At least Palmer worked hard and would help out with the chokers. Jerry didn't do anything except change blocks and stand on the landing trying to talk to Boney to brown nose him. Sam had lost all respect he ever had for him and he knew Jerry was very aware of how felt. Sam was now very careful around him, he did not want to take a chance of making him mad and possibly starting a fight that would get him fired, and that was making him intimidated, but what could he do Jerry was his boss. He really liked his job and wanted to keep it. He still remembered the hard time he had finding a job before he got his job with Boney. So Sam was not really looking forward to that night, but he knew that he and Cheryl needed it. Another worry that he had was that Cheryl did not like people who thought they were self-important, like Jerry, and she would sometimes put them down in a joking but very brave manner. He didn't know how Jerry would take her sense of humor, since he had been taking himself so very seriously since he got his new job. If Jerry said something to her, after one of her remarks, he knew he'd have to do something about it, maybe even punching him in the nose, and that would put his job in jeopardy. She was always putting Sam down in jest when she thought he was acting too macho, but he loved it. He loved her sense of humor and it was always entertaining to him. He wasn't the only one she was always making people laugh with her irreverent sense of humor. So Sam sat there quietly in the back seat with his arm around Cheryl, feeling good but a little tense. He soon spoke up, though, breaking the ice. "What's showing at the movies Jerry?" Jerry watching the road, said. "We don't know. Cindy didn't get the paper today like she usually does. We going to the West Eleventh Drive Inn first, but if we don't like what's playing there we can always go to the Cascade. I'm going to make a beer run at McCoy's before we get out of town." He then made a sharp turn squealing his tires again and then came to an abrupt stop in the parking lot in front of the store. McCoy's, a very small store, with a few very short and narrow isles, but it was located in a very convenient location making it a great place for a beer run before leaving town. It was right on the main artery though town just before you left the city limits. After they stopped, Sam pulled out his wallet and started to hand some money up to Jerry, but Jerry quickly said, "That's alright, Sam, I've got it." He then opened his door and walked into the store. While they were sitting there waiting for Jerry to come back, Cheryl asked Cindy, "Are you from Crescent, Cindy?" Cindy looked back and said. "No, I'm from Albany. That is where all my family is. Its lonely living here when you don't know anyone. Cheryl looked at Sam and said, "Yes I know,"

"Are you from Crescent, Cheryl?"

"No, I'm from Portland." Then Cindy said excitedly. "Oh! I've been to Portland a lot. I really like it. My sister lives there now. We like to go ice skating at Fred Myers. Do you ever go there?"

Yes, I haven't been there in a long time though. I never ice skated. I would break my leg if I did." Sam broke in, laughing, "How very true." Cheryl quickly added. "I have a hard enough time just walking." Sam laughed harder then, knowing how clumsy she could be, and knowing she would not be offended. Jerry walked out of the store holding a paper bag with beer in it. After he got in the car he handed two sixteen ounce cans of Blitz's beer into the back seat for Sam and Cheryl. It was Sam's favorite so he knew then the night couldn't be a complete loss. Jerry revved up his car and they were soon rolling down the Interstate on their way to Eugene, and the West Eleventh Street Drive Inn. After Sam had gotten a good look at Cindy he thought there was no way she could be old enough to have graduated from high school, and looked more like she would be a sophomore or younger if she were in high school. As they drove on to Eugene, she turned to look over the seat again and said to Cheryl, "How come you moved here from Portland?"

"Because of love." Sam turned to look at Cheryl and smiled as she continued; "Now you know what kind of fool I am." Cindy then answered her. "That's not being a fool, Cheryl, that's why I'm in Crescent." Cheryl sounding the wizen old veteran, said, "Cindy, don't ever fall in love. Just use these men for what you want then throw them away. Just sing in the sunshine and then be on your way, like the song says." Sam smiled thinking how unlike Cheryl that really was. Cindy looking at Jerry didn't seem to know what to say, while Jerry stared straight ahead watching his driving, and not saying a word. Sam, as usual, was amused by Cheryl, but wondered how Jerry was taking what she had said. Jerry just asked Sam and Cheryl if they were ready for another one, and when they said they were, he handed two back to them. As fast as Jerry was driving, fast enough to get a ticket, it wasn't long before they were at the Drive-Inn on the far west side of Eugene. As they drove up and were close enough to read the big illuminated sign outside, Jerry said, "It's a Vincent Price movie."

"I like his movies. What about you guys?" Cindy chimed in, "I really like his movies there so scary." Cheryl said she wanted to see the movie and Sam didn't care so it was agreed they would watch the Vincent Price movie. Before the movie as they waited the girls did most of the talking with Cindy doing much of it while Sam and Jerry just drank beer. Cheryl, being older and much more mature than Cindy, seemed to Sam to be acting like her big sister, and it was also obvious to him that they liked each other. After the first movie ended, and while they were waiting for the second to start with the very bright lights, of the Drive-Inn shining into the car. Jerry turned around and said to Sam and Cheryl, "I've got a little weed, do you want to smoke some with us?" Cindy turning around also said, "Come on Cheryl; try some, its good stuff." Cheryl smiled and said, "I smoke weed now and then. I'll try some." Sam just said, "It's alright with me." It was not all right with him and if he had known that Jerry had the weed in his car he never would have came. He took the little whites, but it was marijuana that was all over the news and what the kids in Crescent, who thought they were cool and bad, smoked, and got in trouble with the law for using. He wasn't going to be the only one in the car not to smoke it though. Jerry lit up a short stubby, hand made, cigarette that was twisted to a point on both ends. He pinched one end before sucking on it for all he was worth, and then Cindy did the same before handing the short stubby thing back to Cheryl, who sucked on it loudly, and then she handed it to Sam to smoke. They continued passing it around until they could no more without burning their fingers. Sam didn't feel anything at first, just like he thought, but when he got out of the car to go to the rest room he had a slightly dizzy feeling, and as he walked he started feeling like he was walking above the ground like he was in the air. It made him slow down a little to keep from falling, but he didn't think the feeling was such a great feeling, and it certainly was not going to get him to start smoking marijuana. After he slowly made it back to the car, and when both movies were over they headed back to Crescent. They were all pretty sleepy after watching two long movies, so the car was quiet all the way back home to Crescent with everyone asleep except Jerry. There he let Sam and Cheryl off in front of their apartment and roared off. Sam was tired and very relieved the night was over. Cheryl had found a friend though, and she would see much more of Cindy because she would visit her often making Cheryl's life in Crescent less lonely.

Chapter Seventeen
Sam's Demotion

Things were going along good, but not great, for Sam at work. He liked being the rigging slinger at least most of the time. He had been given the job after Jerry had become hook tender. When it was just him and Stud he enjoyed the job even though it was more work than when Jerry had been helping them. Sam was continuing to find out that he did not like Jerry, but since Jerry was playing hook tender most of the time, he was usually not around to worry about. Palmer, before he got hurt, was able to scout new skid rows, and change the blocks and lines, and still help out with the chokers a lot of the time, especially when it was hard logging. Sam now thought that Jerry was just plain lazy and knew that he could help out with the chokers, when the going was hard, if he wanted to, but just like with Palmer, Sam would rather work harder and not have him around to deal with. He also knew that Boney must know what was going on with Jerry and must accept it so it would do no good to complain to him and that was not Sam's style anyway. Jerry was even able to eventually get Boney to hire a new choker setter, which they did not really need if Jerry would help out with the chokers. Sam knew the big outfits. Like Weyerhaeuser's own logging operations, could afford to have lots of people in the brush, but he doubted a little Jippo logger like Boney could. Bobby, the new choker setter, was a young kid not long out of high school. He was tall, thin, and lanky and wore his long blond hair down to his shoulders like so many kids at the time who were calling themselves hippies. The hostility that had developed against hippies and their wearing of long hair, that was especially bad while Sam was in high school, had softened quite a bit. Sam didn't care about the length of the kid's hair, it didn't bother him. Bobby had never had a real job before, but he had a girl, Stud's step daughter, and since they wanted to get married he knew he had to get a job that paid good money. At first he sat back very shy like, and didn't help much, but it didn't take him long, because Sam was not going to let him do nothing, before he was really helping and working just as hard as Sam and Stud.

Sam had been picking out the turns the way Palmer picked out turns. Palmer had not only taken the good logs but also chunks, and parts of logs over a certain size, and since he had worked with Palmer for such a long time he knew just how big the chunks and pieces had to be to be taken. Palmer had told him that Weyerhaeuser, whose logs they were logging, and whose mill they were sending their logs to, were the ones who wanted the chunks taken off the unit. Since Sam knew it was Weyerhaeuser who paid Boney and it was Boney who paid him he had better keep sending the chunks in. Jerry, though, complained to Sam about sending the chunks in. In the units Jerry had been the Rigging Slinger, and picked out the turns, there had not been many chunks but the unit they were logging then had lots of them. Sam explained to him what Palmer had said about what Weyerhaeuser wanted, and then he just kept sending the chunks and pieces in. He could tell that Jerry did not like it. Although Sam did not like Palmer, he knew he was a smart man; he trusted his judgment and knew he had been taught what to pick up by the Weyerhaeuser people. Jerry would continue to complain about the chunks, but Sam knowing he was right kept sending them in.

About a month after Sam had been made Rigging Slinger the logging crew was finishing up a unit. A logging unit is an area that is marked off for logging usually from a single landing. Many times the unit's Boney logged were taken out of the middle of a large forest of trees, and after it was logged from the air it looked like a patch taken out of a green blanket. The unit's looked pretty bad right after they are logged, but they are soon replanted and it is not long before they are green again and filled with little trees. The animal population actually increases after the harvest of the trees because they are able to eat the brush and small trees that are able to grow after the big sun blocking trees are gone. Down in the valley's the Indians used to burn the forests to increase the deer population.

The crew was finishing up the last few turns on the last logging road when Jerry came up to Sam and abruptly, while pointing at one of the spinning blocks at the bottom of the hill, said "There is a big slab down there by the block. See it down there?" Sam looked down at the block that was strapped to a huge stump and was bouncing up and down as the haul back line kept running through it as a turn of logs was being dragged onto the landing. There by the block, he saw a large reddish-yellow slab of wood that had been split from a tree. It was about fourteen feet long and had enough wood in it that Sam thought it should be taken. After looking at it Sam said, "Yea, I see it." Giving Jerry the same attitude that he had given him. Then Jerry said, "I want you to leave it. You can reach out and get that small log behind it, but leave the slab." Sam didn't say a word but he knew the slab should be taken, but he also knew it would be useless to say a thing so he just stared at the slab. Jerry continued, "I'm going to go up and talk to Boney, and by the time I get back you should have that small log sent in and then we'll send the blocks in. He started to walk away but stopped and turned around to look at Sam and say, "Make sure you leave that slab down there." Sam, just said, "Okay." Then Jerry turned around and started climbing up the hill to the landing. Sam didn't like his tone of voice and attitude, but he had already decided that he would put up with him to keep his job so he said nothing more in reply. After Jerry left though he could feel the adrenaline rise in his veins and as he stood there staring at the slab, getting angrier by the moment, he decided he would send the slab in. "To hell with Jerry," he said to himself, "the thing needs to go in." He thought that it stood out like a sour thumb and he knew if a Weyerhaeuser man, one of those guys they always saw riding around in their yellow company pickups saw it, and Sam thought he couldn't miss it, he would make them come back and pick it up, and what an extra expense that would be for Boney. Sam stopped the rigging in front of him then unhooked one of the chokers from the Butt Rigging and hooked it to the end of the other choker so he would have enough length to reach out and hook the small log. He then pulled the end of the two hooked together chokers all the way to the small log and choked it. Then he sent the small log slowly in, but when it got close to the slab he stopped the rigging. Stud looked at him wondering what he was doing. He then hooked the choker on the log to the Butt Rigging, and then took the other choker and set it on the Slab. Stud looked at him funny he had been close enough to hear what Jerry had said to him. Sam just stared ahead, not looking at stud, as he got out of the way and sent the slab and log into the landing. Sam watched them run up the hill into the landing and then whistled for the haywire. It always takes a while for them to hook up the haywire, on the landing, and send it slowly back into the brush so it won't come apart. So Sam stood there in the light of a beautiful morning sun, relaxed and waiting for the haywire. He let the fact that he wasn't supposed to have sent the slab in slip to the back of his mind so while Sam was standing there looking up at the landing, happy that they had finished logging the unit. Jerry came charging up to him yelling, "Why did you send that slab in! I told you I did not want you to send it in. You spent all that time reaching out for that slab and they are just going to throw it off the landing. At first Sam said nothing, knowing he was guilty, so Jerry kept yelling at him. "I'm the hook tender here. I tell you what to do, and when I tell you not to take a slab you don't take it. That slab was not worth shit. You cost Boney a lot of money wasting time reaching out and getting that slab." Sam, finally getting irritated, said with a raised voice, "When I got down to the slab, and got a good look at it, I could tell it was big enough to take! If we leave that thing Weyerhaeuser will make us come back and get it. Then Boney will lose some big time money. Jerry yelling again, said, "That slab was not big enough. Boney and I could tell from the landing it was not big enough. Jerry mentioning Boney got Sam worrying about his job, but he thought surely he would not fire him over that slab. Sam had been worried enough, though, to let Jerry yell at him. Before walking away in a huff Jerry said, "Send the blocks in and come on into the landing. Sam stood there mad that he had let a wimp like Jerry talk to him like that, and not do a thing about it. He knew he had to keep his job no matter what though, but he felt like a whipped dog as he walked down to the blocks. With his face tightened, he would not say a thing to Stud or Bobby, both of whom had heard him get chewed out, as they hooked up the blocks to the haywire and then followed them in as they bounced up the hill. When Sam got to the landing, everyone was busy getting things ready to move to the next unit including Boney. Sam was a little worried but Boney never said a thing to him. He did lose his whistle as Jerry made the new guy, Bobby, the Rigging Slinger. Sam still had his good paying job, but he knew that he was not going to be able to work with Jerry, and he was going to find a new job if it killed him. Later Sam would be vindicated. On the very next unit Weyerhaeuser made them go back over half the unit where Jerry had been picking out the logs and leaving the chunks as he tried to teach Bobby what to take and what to leave. Sam had done the right thing, but he did not get the Rigging Slinger job back.

CHAPTER EIGHTEEN
THE LETTER'S

One Friday, a couple of weeks later, Sam was looking out a window of the Crummy as it was driving into the parking lot of his apartment when he noticed that his car was missing from it's parking place. That was unusual because Cheryl had always been home waiting for him when he got off work. When he climbed out of the Crummy, carrying his cork boots and lunch pail, he was not overly concerned about the car being gone though. He knew they needed groceries so he just thought Cheryl was simply at the grocery store, and would be back soon He entered the apartment and walked over to the refrigerator to get a cold drink, and sitting here on the kitchen table, underneath a salt shaker, was a note from Cheryl. He picked it up and started reading it, calmly at first. Cheryl had written on the note that she had taken his car to Portland, and if he wanted it he would have to come and get it. Completely surprised and dumbfounded, Sam read on and found out why she had left. She had found the letters that he had been getting from Brenda. The ones that he thought he had hidden so carefully and the ones he wished that he had burned in his mothers old wood stove. Although he had not told Brenda that he was coming back to her, she thought he would, and as the weeks had gone by, he had helped her think that way. So in her letters she mentioned him coming back to her. Now Cheryl had read those letters. He felt that she must hate him now, believing that he was going to leave her, and that is not what he planned to do. He was going to give their life together a good chance, and he was not even close to leaving her, he loved her. He did have to admit, though, that he had thoughts about it on those evenings he spent reading Brenda's letters at his folk's house.

It was a Friday, but not pay day and he was broke as he so often was on the Friday between pay days. So he would not be able to buy a bus ticket to pick up; his car until the following Friday when he got paid. So he settled down to a lonely week. His small two-bedroom apartment seemed large without Cheryl there to keep him company.

That first night, as he lay in bed by himself, he remembered that stormy night that she had come to live with him, and how he had warmed her cold body with his. How very much he had loved her then, and how happy he was to see her especially after he thought that she had decided to leave him. He loved her still and missed her so very much. He knew he would be going back to Brenda and Patrick, now that Cheryl had read Brenda's letters, and no matter how much that made him feel good, it did not ease the ache in his heart that losing Cheryl was causing him.

The next week went by slowly with Sam beginning to hate his job because he still was not getting along with Jerry, and with him missing Cheryl especially at the end of the day when he went home to his lonely apartment. Friday, and payday finally did come for Sam and the following day he got up early, for a Saturday, and started walking to the bus station. It was a cold, dry, dark winter morning with the sky a gray blanket over Sam's head as he walked along under the tall trees with their ugly, scraggily, limbs bare of leaves. His wind breaker jacket cut the cold wind that made his cheeks sting, as he walked quickly along the sidewalks and across streets with his hands jammed down hard into his pockets. Walking so quickly, he was almost running, he soon made it to the warmth of the bus station. The room, with a large window facing the street, was empty except for the lady at the counter. After he bought his ticket he settled down to reading a newspaper. Soon though a loud squeal of a bus breaking broke his concentration as his bus pulled to a hard stop in front of the small station, and then he was quickly loaded onto the bus, and was on his way lying back comfortably in a seat. The bus arrived in Portland at a very large and busy bus terminal. Sam left the bus and quickly found a long row of pay phones. He dialed the number Cheryl had written on the note. He was feeling very sad and guilty as he waited for her to answer. Guilty because she had been living with him and told her he was going to marry her, yet he had been writing his wife telling her that he loved and missed. Let alone the fact that he had started seeing her when he was married and got her pregnant causing her to get an abortion. He knew she would surely hate him and that she should hate him. He deserved her hate. He heard the voice that he loved answer the phone. Sam answered quickly and nervously. "This is Sam. I've come to get my car." Cheryl answered him calmly, and with no anger in her voice, which surprised him and pleased him, "Where are you?"

"I'm at the Greyhound Bus Station here in down town Portland. Then Cheryl said. "I'll be by in your car in about thirty minutes. Wait for me in front of the bus station. I'll park the car across the street from the station." Sam then said, "Okay," Speaking just above a whisper. Cheryl hung up leaving Sam feeling just a bit better because she had not sounded like she hated him like he thought she would.

He walked through the crowd of people at the bus station with the sounds of the announcer, calling out the times of the departing buses, filling the huge, cavernous, room. Sam had always thought bus stations were interesting places. He was a people watcher, and in a big city bus station there were all kinds of people to watch. There were young people and old people, big and small people, and people dressed well and people dressed shabbily. Sam sat there watching them on one of the large, and very long, wooden benches, which Sam thought in its life time had to have been the seat to thousands and thousands of people. He often turned from watching the milling crowd to glance at the big clock hanging on the wall; He did not want to Miss Cheryl's arrival. Sitting there, Sam thought of how much a bus station was the like the airports he had been to in his life. The people at the very few airports he had waited in, including the one in Portland, were dressed better and carried more expensive luggage, but he couldn't help seeing how the two places were alike, except for the very obvious difference in the people's status in life. The airports certainly didn't have the homeless characters, in their ragged clothes, that he saw hanging around the bus station, but he even enjoyed watching them, as they now and then begged for money from the people who passed by them. Sam sat across from a couple of young kids who he thought must have been college students. A boy and a girl, and both had long hair down to their shoulders, the girls being very blond, and the boy's hair not so blond. They had leather bands tied around their heads holding their hair in place. Their cloths were made of leather with beads sown on them in Indian designs and they were wearing moccasins. Sam had seen hippies wearing the same type of clothes but the Indian costumes these kids were wearing looked new and expensive, not like the much worn leather clothes he had often seen hippies wear. They looked like rich kids playing at being Indians or hippies.

Sam looked at the big clock on the wall again, and then stopped his idle wondering because it was almost time for Cheryl to arrive. So he hurried outside making his way through the crowd. It wasn't long after he was outside that she was parking his car on the other side of the street from where he was standing. He was very glad to see her as he walked across the street, but he wondered how she was going to act towards him. As he approached the car, she scooted over to the passenger side allowing him to get in behind the steering wheel. He again felt guilty and tense as he sat there beside her, and she said nothing after she told him he needed to take her to Sandy's house. As he drove off down the street, she continued to sit there quietly on her side of the car, which caused him to feel even more guilty and more uncomfortable. He knew there was nothing he could say that could explain away the letters, so he didn't even try. Cheryl continued to say nothing as Sam drove on slowly between the tall skyscrapers, he was in no hurry. Sam, with the pain showing so plainly on his face realizing that he was seeing her for the last time, was almost ready to cry. He looked over at her but she just stared ahead, breaking his heart. He almost wished that she would yell at him and call him names just so she wouldn't just sit there and say nothing. After Sam had driven for a while, though, she did say something, Calmly Cheryl said simply, "How are you Sam?" Relieved, Sam said, "I'm fine. How are you Cheryl?" It's good to see you again." Continuing in the same calm tone of voice Cheryl said, "How could you do it Sam? How could you live with me and then write to your wife and tell her that you loved her and that you wanted to come back to her. You were telling me all that time that you loved me and wanted to marry me. How could you do it?" The words were hitting him like fists. What could he say though there were no good excuses? With tears in his eye's he said, "Cheryl, I love you. I love you so very much."

"How could you love me and do what you did?"

"I still love my wife and son and don't want to hurt them."

"What do you think you are doing to me? So what are you going to do? Are you going, back to your wife?" He had decided to go back to his wife, but that was when he thought he had lost Cheryl. Now though, he was beginning to be unsure that he was going to lose her and so he said, "I don't know Cheryl. I just don't know." Sam felt it was good that she was talking to him even if she was angry at him and he had wondered if she would let him see her again. If she had read his letter she would know that he still loved her and had not planned to leave her. He knew that she had been hurt but felt that she still cared about him. That is something he felt that he should have known. She had shown her love for him many times before. How could she have quit loving him so quickly? The car had turned quiet again as Cheryl sat on her side of the car looking as sad as Sam. Sam had decided that he was not going to just walk away from her without at least trying to stop her. So once they got into Jackie's neighborhood Sam turned off into a small park they had visited a few times before. As soon as he turned, Cheryl said, "Don't Sam. I want to go to Jackie's."

"Cheryl, I just want to talk to you for a few minutes. I will never see you again; can't I just talk to you for a little while?" Cheryl didn't answer, so Sam went ahead and parked the car. After he parked the car, Cheryl said, "What do you want to say Sam?" Sam was so sure that she still loved him then that he believed if he could just hold her everything would be alright. So he scooted over next to her, but she continued to stare ahead and said, "Sam don't." She said it softly without conviction so he put his arm around her and said, "Cheryl, you do know that I love you and I will always love you." He then pulled her to him and kissed her. Cheryl did not resist and kissed him back. After a long kiss she turned away from him though and again said, "Don't Sam." Sam backed away and with tears in his eyes he wailed. "I'm so sorry for what I've done to you, but I do love you and I can't stand the thought of never seeing you again. Cheryl, I 'm so sorry for what I did. I am truly an ass. When I told my wife I was leaving her and wanted a divorce I thought I didn't love her. I love you and that is why I left her though. I did not hurt you on purpose. That is the last thing I want to do. When my wife wrote me the first letter telling me that she still loved me and wanted me back, I did not write her back for a long time. Then when you didn't want to live with me and I realized how I missed her and Patrick. I started writing her back and telling her that I loved her because I still do care about her, but I thought I was losing you. So she has continued to write me and I have continued to write her back. Cheryl I love you and I want you to love me. I can't help my self I will always love you." While Sam was speaking, Cheryl sat there very still beside him, with her head bowed down, staring at the floor avoiding looking at him. When he stopped, she said while not moving. "So you do still love your wife?"

"Yes, but I will never stop loving you, though, and I never want to be without you, and now that you don't hate me. I don't know if I will be going back to my wife. It is true I thought I would be." Then he turned his head to look at her closely and said, "I do know that I love you so very much." She then turned her head to him and came willingly into his arms as he put them around her and they kissed and continued to kiss, and for the first time that day Sam knew for sure that he was not losing Cheryl. It was not long before they were making glorious love. After their love making they sat happily together, Cheryl sitting snuggly against Sam. They had gone through so much in a few short hours, but they were back together. They decided that Sam would leave Cheryl at Jackie's after they left the park but he would come back the following weekend and then they would spend the whole weekend together. While he held Cheryl close to him, Sam started his car and drove to Jackie's where he did not mind seeing her leave knowing that he would see her again very soon.

Chapter Nineteen
California

Things went along smoothly with Sam for awhile at least. At work things were still tense with Jerry, but he was getting along all right with the rest of the crew. Bobby, the new Rigging Slinger was turning out to be a good worker, and a good kid. Sam was missing his family, but he would visit his mother's house often, and read the letter's Brenda was sending him every week, and he would continue to send her a letter every time he got one from her. He even started calling her on the phone, talking to her and little Patrick. He was also able to see Cheryl almost every weekend and their love making was always very intense after he had almost lost her. To him she was the best friend he had ever had in his life. He could not imagine his life without her, yet after a couple of months of her not living with him he was telling his wife that he would quit his job and drive down to New Mexico to be with her, and little Patrick just as soon as he could save enough money, and he was very serious about it even if it meant leaving Cheryl no matter how much he loved her. He had made up his mind again he wanted to be with his family. Saving the money was not easy for him with his bills and all the trips he was taking to Portland, with the cost of taking Cheryl out, and when he stayed over the weekend, the cost of a motel room many times for both Friday and Saturday nights. He just could not stay away from her though, and she was always there ready for him, every time he wanted to see her with just as much love for him as he had for her. She was like a drug habit that he could not break. He so enjoyed her company, and would stretch out his visits as long as he could, and of course he was addicted to their wild sex. She was also buying the little white crosses for them, and he was taking one almost every day.

There was to be an abrupt change though.

Sam was sitting on the couch one evening at his folk's house watching their favorite television show, Gunsmoke, when the phone rang. After answering the phone his mother gave it to him saying that John, his brother, was on the phone. John was living in California logging for their Uncle Mike. After getting the phone Sam said. "Hi, John how are you doing?" The call was unexpected because Sam and John hardly ever talked to each other. They had fought all the time while they were growing up, and it had carried over to their grown up years. Sam loved his brother, though, and thought that John loved him in his own way. John answered Sam in the gruff tone that he always used. "I'm doing all right. How are you doing?"

"I'm great. How's the logging going there in California?" Then John, getting quickly to the point, asked Sam very unexpectedly. "Fine, how much are you making working for Patton?"

"Four dollars and twenty cents an hour." Why?"

"We need choker setters here. We had two guys quit. Mike is paying choker setters five dollars an hour, and we're been working six days a week, ten hours a day. Making over five dollars and hour and all the overtime we are working you can make a lot more than you're making working for Patton." Sam immediately thought that it would be a perfect way to leave a job he no longer wanted, and make money for his trip to New Mexico. So he said, "When would I have to be down there?"

"We need someone right now. I'm the only one on the chokers."

"Man That is bad. Are you logging with a Cat or a Yarder?"

"A Yarder." Sam would have liked to have a little more time to make up his mind but he didn't have it, and since John was the only one on the chokers he thought he should help him. He was his brother after all, and he did want to leave his job with Patton, and save money for his trip. Making more money in California would make saving easier. So he said to John, "Okay, how do I get to where you're logging now?"

"Just take I-5 down to Redding and just before you get to Redding turn off onto 19 to Pine Grove. When you get to Pine Grove you turn east on Highway 87 into the mountains and after about fifteen miles you'll come to "High Mountain Lodge" and that is where we're staying. Just ask at the desk and they'll tell you where the Adam's logging Company's, cabin is."

"All right John, I'll pack up tonight and leave tomorrow morning. I'll see you tomorrow night."

"Okay, Sam, I'll see you tomorrow."

"Sam got up early the next morning, before light, at the same time that he always got up to go to work. He had just moved in with his folks, to save money, so his mother had breakfast ready for him. He ate it quickly, anxious to get started on his trip, and said goodbyes to his mother and stepfather. He threw his suitcases into his little blue Chevy Nova, that he had just bought, and drove it down to the gas station where he had been going to catch the Crummy for work. Jerry had stopped driving the Crummy to his apartment to pick him up because things were getting very tense between them. So Sam had been driving down to the Texaco Station, in the middle of town, and leaving his car to catch the Crummy there. It had just given him another reason to dislike Jerry. Sam wanted to make sure that he told Boney in person that he was going to quit. He had always appreciated getting the job, and that Boney had always been a decent guy to work for. He parked his car and walked over to the Crummy, which had just driven up to the gas pumps. As Sam walked to the Crummy, he could see Jerry's face tighten as he spotted him, just like his face so often did when he was around Jerry. He knew Jerry wondered why he was approaching him instead of just getting in the Crummy, but he didn't care what he thought. Sam quickly said. "Is Boney stopping here today?" Jerry didn't say anything. He just sat there in the Crummy. Sam knew he didn't want to answer him because he had become such an ass , and Jerry had to know he despised him, and had lost complete respect for him. Sam just stood there waiting for an answer. Jerry finally said looking behind him, "He's right behind us. There he is now." Boney drove his dark maroon pick-up by them and parked it beside Sam's car. Sam turned around and started walking over to Boney's pick-up feeling on edge from being around Jerry, and knowing it was a very good thing he was never going to see him again. He was angry, but a little nervous because he had never talked to Boney except for a few times before and had seen his temper flare many times. Boney was still sitting in his pick-up when Sam got to it. Sam quickly said, "I've got to quit Boney. I'm going to work with my brother in California. It is a better deal for me." Boney turned to look at him for a second. Seeming to get angry, he boomed, "A better deal!" He knew that Boney would not like that he was quitting. He was needed, but he had not expected that reaction. He quickly answered getting a little irate himself. I'll be making more money. I'll be paid much more per hour and get lots of overtime." Then, without another word, Sam turned around and walked back to his car and drove away; glad to be done with it.

He'd cooled down by the time he hit I-5 and started feeling very good about leaving a job he wanted to leave so badly. He was excited too and a little fearful like he always was when he started a new job, and like when he went off to college, and the service. As he drove on the highway through the tree covered rolling hills, south of Crescent he felt freer than he had felt in a long time. It was an adventure and he liked the feeling. He drove south by the oak thickets that covered the hills to Roseburg, and then through the rolling hills a sea of brown from the tall dried out grass that covered them to Myrtle Creek, where he used to visit his Grandfathers farm when he was a kid. It brought back wonderful memories of his summer visits to their farm. Then he drove up into the hills covered with Fir trees, and down again into Medford and then way up and over the high pass through the Siskiyou Mountains into Northern California. After he crossed the border, it wasn't long before he was turning east into the high Mountains and forests of the Northeastern corner of California.

Climbing on a two lane, very steep road, that if he had driven off of he would have fallen forever. He drove high into the Mountains above Pine Grove until he came to large flat plateau. On the climb up, the steep mountains were mostly bare, but the plateau was like an oasis in the mountains. A large beautiful blue lake shimmered in the sunlight surrounded by large pine trees and greenery. Sam slowed down to look at the surprising sight, able to take it easy on a road that was now flat. As he continued, the road wound its way through a forest of huge and very tall pine trees, back among them he could see here and there small log cabins, and always on the lakeside the blue of the mountain lake between the trees. He eventually came upon a large log building looking out on the lake. Sam hoped it would be the place he was looking for, and the building did have a large wooden sign standing in plain sight in front of it that had "High Mountain Lodge" written on it. So Sam very glad his trip was over drove into the parking lot and stopped. Just as he stopped a white pick-up pulled in beside him. As he got out and started walking to the lodge the man in the pick-up got out and started walking up to him. Sam thought the man looked familiar and then the man said as he neared him, "Are you Sam?" He knew then that it had to be his Uncle Mike and as he had gotten closer he had recognized him even though he had not seen him in many years. "Yes, Uncle Mike, it's me Sam. How are you?"

"I'm fine Sam." Your mother called and said you were coming. She told me what time you left, and I figured you would be getting here just about now."

"I thought John was going to be here to meet me?"

"John is not here. He got a call last night from his ex-wife and took off this morning saying he would be back next weekend. Very surprised, Sam said, "What? John's not here? He told me on the phone that he was going to be here."

"He had planned on being here Sam, but that ex-wife has him running to her for some reason. I told him that he is not married to her anymore but he went anyway. It's like they never got a divorce."

"How are we going to log with just me on the chokers?"

"I've hired a young kid. He's never set chokers before, but I think he will make a good choker setter. I think he will be a hard worker." Sam was worried because he knew Mike would expect him to change logging roads now, and although he had helped change logging roads hundreds of times he had never lined up the new roads and picked out the stumps to put the blocks on. He was mad at John for putting him in such a predicament. The old rivalry between them was coming back to him. He had quit his job in Oregon and there was no going back so he knew he had to keep this job especially if he was ever going to get the money to get back to his family, but he was still very mad at John. Sam followed Mike's pickup to a small cabin hidden among the trees. John had told him before there were cabins for the tourist, but they rented a few to Mike for his logging crew. The cabin was nice; it had a couple of bed rooms, a stove and a refrigerator. Mike gave him the keys and told him he would be by to pick him up at six in the morning. Then he drove off to Pine Grove where he was staying. John had left plenty of food for him so he wouldn't go hungry. That night, as Sam lay in bed trying to fall asleep, in a strange bed, he was feeling very insecure about his new job. He had found John's alarm clock and set it so he was awake when his Uncle Mike got there in the morning. They only had to drive thirty minutes on a flat, gravel road before they came to the landing. When they drove onto the landing, Sam saw the shortest, funniest looking, Yarder Tower, that he had ever seen in his life. It was not round and tall like Patton's or any other tower that he had ever seen in his life. It was short and square and about half the height of Boney's Tower, and it tilted making it look very strange indeed to Sam. He knew that as short as it was, it would not give any lift to the chokers, so the chokers would always be dragging on the ground getting all tangled so he would always have to be untangling them before they could be set making his job twice as hard. He did not say anything knowing that his Uncle Mike had to have been the one who bought the sorry looking thing. There was a big fire going on the landing when they arrived. There were three men huddled around it keeping warm. Sam's Uncle Mike got out of the pick up while Sam put on his cork boots and then started walking to the warm fire when a beat up old pick-up came rattling onto the landing. A kid, maybe a couple of years out of high school got out and started walking towards the fire. Mike introduced Sam to the Crew and the new young choker setter Billy. Sam was not impressed with his choker setter. The boy was very thin and looked weak to him, but Sam remembered that he had thought Stud would never be any real help setting chokers when he first saw him. He could not believe that the kid was not even wearing boots. He was wearing tennis shoes. He was going to have a lot of pressure being the rigging slinger, and now having to change logging roads, and the only help he was going to have was an inexperienced kid. Worried, Sam strapped the belt that held the whistle, around his waist and headed into the brush with his choker setter close behind. He walked down to where they finished logging the day before. He then remembered that he didn't have to put up with Jerry anymore. That put a smile on his face and helped him forget about his worries for a while. As they stood there in the cold, waiting for the chokers to show up, Sam said to Billy, "Mike told me that you've never set chokers before."

"No, I never have."

"It's not hard. I'll show you how a choker works when they get here. You just have to set it as quick as you can, and work hard all day and you'll be all right. What kind of work have you done before?"

"The last job I had was making portable buildings."

"How much did that pay?"

"Two dollars and fifty cents and hour."

"Wow, you'll be making more than two dollars more and hour on this job." Billy looking surprised said, "I'm going to be making four fifty an hour?"

"Yea, that's what Mike told me. You need to get you some steel toed boots just as soon as you can, or you'll get your toes squashed. Mike told me they don't wear cork boots up here like mine, so I guess you don't need to buy a pair of those. I'm going to keep wearing mine though. Looking at Sam's boots, Billy said, "Those are great boots you have. I like the spikes on the bottom. I've been out of work for a couple of months but just as soon as I can afford it, I'm going to buy some boots. My wife works, but we just had a baby so she hasn't been working. We are very short on money right now." Sam, feeling sorry for him, said, "You really needed this job didn't you?" "Yes, I did." They heard a loud horn blast come from the Yarder as Sam jerked on his whistle and then the large cable stretched in front of them lifted a little and started to swing up and down as it began pulling the chokers down from the landing. Before the chokers got to them, Sam said, "Now, always watch that big cable in front of you, and don't ever walk under it while it's moving. It can drop down and squash you head so that it is even with your shoulders. Always remember it not only goes up and down but it can also swing sideways if it get's hung on something and then comes loose. If you have to walk underneath either the main line or the haul back when it's not moving always look up at it while you walking under it and hurry. The mainline is this line in front of us and the haul back is that smaller line on the other side of it. Never get right under a turn of logs when they are going up the hill either. A choker could break and a log can come back down the hill at you or the logs in the turn can hit another log, big rock, or a root wad, that's a stump that been pulled out of the ground, and they can come down the hill at you. Always get way out of the way after you have set your choker so that nothing can hit you when the logs start moving, those logs can bounce around. Always watch the limbs they don't always cut them off, and they can kill you just as quick as a log can. Just follow me today. I'll show you where to go." Billy watched Sam and listened carefully to him while he was talking. Sam could see that he had a mouth full of rotten teeth and thought again that he really needed this job. As the day went on, Sam found that Billy a fast, willing learner, and worked hard. He hustled to the chokers and was stronger that he looked. Sam had to warn him a few times when he was not far enough out of the way to be safe, but that was part of his job and he knew the kid would learn. He found that he liked him. Sam was thankful that he did not have to change logging roads that day, and by the end of the day, felt better knowing that he had a good choker setter working with him.

The next day they finished the logging road they had been working on. Sam's with Billy's good help, was able to move the blocks and set up the new road with the haywire without any trouble. After the first road change Sam was feeling much better about his move to California. He found he was really enjoying his new job, and time at work was going by faster than he thought because he was using his head more now. With the picking out of the logs and making the road changes, and teaching Billy about setting chokers his mind was much busier than when he worked in Oregon. The ten-hour days, he was working, did not feel any longer than the eight-hour days he was working before. In the evening it was a little lonely for him in the log cabin by himself. He had never been in a log cabin before and he thought it was pretty cool though. He had enough food for his evening meals and to make his lunches, and Mike told him he would bring him groceries when he ran out. He was working his long day, having his meal as soon as he got to the cabin, and going to sleep really to tired to do any thing else. In the brush, Sam thought that he was doing all right. He was getting logs into the landing and loaded trucks down the hill, and Mike never complained about the job he was doing, and he had forgotten about his worries about not being able to do the job, with the help of a good choker setter. He was content and getting more confident with his job every day.

The loneliness started getting to him after a while though so he started calling Brenda on a phone that they had in the cabin, talking to her and Patrick. He would always tell them that he loved them, and that he would be coming to them soon. When he had called Brenda the first time he heard her sadly answer, "Hello Sam, I miss you so much. When are you coming back to Patrick and me?" That made him yearn for her so much as he answered her, "Just as soon as I have enough money. I have this great job now, in California, and I am now making enough money to come to you. It will not be long now two or three months at the most."

"You know that I need you Sam?"

"I need you and I need Patrick and it won't be long now."

"It is too long Sam you can't come now?"

"I don't have the money. I really don't. I want to see you just as much as you want to see me. I am working just as hard as I can to make enough money to come to you and Patrick. I love you two so very much. Then he sadly said goodbye, and hung up and went to sleep.

He also sometimes called Cheryl not as often as he called Brenda, though. Some nights he would lay in his cot staring at the ceiling and start thinking about Cheryl and even though he knew for sure he was going to go back to Brenda he would just have to pick up the phone and start dialing. One night he called and heard the voice he was so familiar with and loved as Cheryl answered, and he said "Hello it's just me."

"Hello Sam,"

"Thought I would call and see how your doing."

"I'm doing fine just here watching television. I'm baby sitting my nephews. I got to go to one of their soccer games today. It was fun."

"That's great. I'm glad you're having a good time."

"I wouldn't go that far Sam."

"Well I'm not even near to having a good time. Here all by my lonesome. I just work ten hours a day and eat and sleep. That's my day. I sure miss you. You don't think that you could come down here and visit me. It is a great place. People must spend a lot of money to stay in these cabins during the summer. There are big trees all around and big lake right next door."

"Sam, where would I get the money?" I have been looking for a job though, and I think I might be close to getting one."

"That's good, but I sure could use some company down here, though, and you could bring me some of those white crosses. I running out and they sure keep me going."

"You know I would love to come down there and be your kept woman and provide you with all the white crosses that you would ever want."

"If I keep working down here, getting all the hours I'm getting now, I could really afford to keep you as my kept woman." Then getting serious he said, "Cheryl you know that I still plan on saving enough money to go to New Mexico." The phone was quiet then, but he knew that Cheryl did not really believe that he was leaving especially after he had come back to her the last time after she had taken his car, and how after that he had visited her in Portland almost every weekend until he went to California. It would be hard for him he knew, but he had really made up his mind, and knew he would go back to his family, but he said "I don't know how long it will take, but the first thing I'm going to do just as soon as I have enough money is to come to Portland to see you, and that you can count on."

"I'm counting on that. When will it be?"

"Just as soon as I can. It shouldn't be too long. I'll take a weekend off soon. I'm getting sleepy now. I am about ready to pass out. Got to get up at five. I'll call you in couple of days and I will see you soon Cheryl. Goodbye."

"Goodbye Sam."

Sam's brother, John, finally showed up after he had worked in California for about two weeks and Sam was very glad to see him. He had long forgotten that he was angry at him. They had almost finished the unit they were logging, and were about to move. So Sam, as usual when it came to logging, did not think that he was experienced enough to make the move. He would have to take the guy lines down, and find and notch the stumps for them at the new location. The locations of the guy lines were very important because they were the lines that supported the tower keeping it from falling down. He would also have to figure out where to put the blocks for the first road they were to log. He knew he was no hook tender yet. He was doing the job, but was glad that it would not be his responsibility anymore. John took over right away, just as he always liked it, and Sam was glad to let him. The moving of the Yarder and the hooking up of the guy lines went very easily making Sam wonder why he worried. Then after they were done he knew he could have done it. He was very satisfied, though, just being the rigging slinger. They started getting more logs out now that there were three of them on the chokers which put Sam's Uncle Mike in a very good mood.

At the end of John's first week on the job, they were setting chokers on some flat ground a long way from the Yarder that stood on a high hump. There, because of the shortness of the Yarder Tower and the flatness of the ground, the chokers were coming back to the logging crew, not held in the air, but bouncing along the ground. Sam had thought because of the flatness of the ground that it should have been logged with Cats or Caterpillar He knew Boney would have logged the unit with Cats that is if Weyerhaeuser would have let him. Every time that the chokers came back they had to take the time to untangle them, and the stiff chokers were getting so coiled from running on the ground they looked like the end of a corkscrew. They were very hard to pull through the brush that way, and would catch on every little limb, bush, or twig. They were in the corner of a unit and to reach out to the very end of that corner, to get the logs there, they had to log over a rise. From behind the rise they could not even see the top of the short tower on the Yarder. Sam knew the chokers would have to run on the ground over the hump so the main line might run off to the right side of the hump as it went into the landing and get hooked behind a stump. If it did when the Yarder pulled hard, to get over the stump, the main line would come off the stump and then it would swing over towards them. With that worry in mind, Sam walked way out of the way every time he sent a turn of logs in. One time he thought the logs were not running straight to the Yarder, like the main line was hooked behind a stump, but he could not tell for sure since he could not see the tower. He had walked far enough away to think he was safe and he had made Billy walk even farther away. Sam walked back closer to the line, though, to see if he could see the turn of logs being dragged in. He thought that even if the line was to come over towards him it would catch on something on the high hump after it came off the stump.

John was off checking out the new logging road so he was safe. Sam kept his eyes on the big cable stretched so tight in front of him ready to run if he thought it was going to come over at him. The main line tightened even more and the big engine on the Yarder roared as it strained to pull the logs loose from a stump. Sam was caught, he knew the line was coming over now, but he did not think it could reach over as far as he was standing, but he crouched down ready to jump just in case. The main line tightened again and the Yarder engine roared as it tried to pull the logs loose from the stump that was holding them. Sam heard the Yarder roar again and again as it strained harder and harder to pull the logs loose. The big cable lifted in front of him stretching tight and reaching him about chest high and only twenty yards away. He knew he should have been further out of the way and also thinking that he was starting to act like Palmer who liked to press his luck by being to close. Then he heard the chokers snap and what he dreaded happened. The big line in front of him started swinging towards him. He dove to the ground thinking he was a dead man, knowing for sure that he could not dive faster than that line was swinging. It whizzed over the top of him and then swung back over him as he hugged the ground eating dirt. Lucky for him the line straightened out then and started running where it was suppose to run far away from where the prone Sam lay.

He stayed glued to the ground and would not even lift his head to look thinking the big line might swing back at him, but it did not the big Yarder had pulled it straight. Sam eventually rose to his feet thinking he was one lucky logger until he looked around and saw mike lying on the ground. The big line had reached over far enough to hit Billy, after it had swung over his head. Sam rushed over to him thinking he had been hurt bad, and feeling guilty thinking that it was his fault for not getting both of them farther away from the main line. Before he got there, Billy jumped up and Sam could see that he was okay except his mouth was bloody where he was holding it, and when he got to there Billy showed him a few of his rotten teeth that had been knocked out of his mouth. Sam was very relieved knowing it could have been much worse. He had forgotten about the close call that had happened to him as he examined Billy's mouth. He could only see a small cut and the broken teeth, but he knew his jaw could be broken, and he also knew that Billy had been very lucky because the main line must have reached it's farthest, on its swing, just before it swung back, when it hit him, or it would have been much worse. Sam whistled the eight long eerie whistles, that broke the silence of the quiet woods, and that signaled an injured logger. The landing crew rushed out with a stretcher, but Billy walked into the landing insisting he was alright. Mike had called for an Ambulance so it wasn't long after they reached the landing that one arrived and headed down the hill with Billy to the Pine Grove Hospital. After the Ambulance left, Mike drove a solemn Sam and John to their cabin while Sam explained to him what had happened. Sam was feeling guilty about the accident as they drove still thinking that he should have kept him and Billy farther away from the line.

The next morning Mike told them that he had visited Billy in the hospital and the doctor told him that, except for the broken teeth, he would be fine. The company insurance was going to pay for fixing his teeth and he would be back to work after his teeth were fixed. That made Sam feel a lot better knowing that Billy was going to be alright and he was going to get his teeth fixed to boot.

Then it was just Sam and brother John on the chokers. Sam could not believe how smoothly it went with just the two of them. They got plenty of logs out and what was surprising to Sam was they actually got along, and not only that but he was making such great money, but the good times were not to last.

One morning, not to long after the accident, and while they were waiting around the fire, getting toasted before they headed down into the brush, it started snowing. That didn't bother Sam. He knew that he could work in the snow, he had done it before. It was not snowing hard just giant, dry, flakes wafting slowly down the sky and sticking tight to the frozen dry ground. There was just a thin coating of snow on the ground as they walked down to the chokers making tracks in the snow as they walked. When they got to the chokers, John said, "Don't be surprised if Mike calls us into the landing soon." Sam, surprised looked at him and said, "Why?" Then John said matter of factually. "We could get snowed out for the rest of the winter."

"What! How could we be snowed out? I've worked in snow above my knees before."

"We're at a very high altitude, even higher than where you worked. They get snowed out every year at about this time. Once it starts snowing around here it keeps snowing and it gets deep fast, above your head. There have been years it started snowing and Mike didn't get his equipment out fast enough and had to leave his equipment up here all winter in the snow. Mike may be calling for the low-boy right now to pick up the loader and Yarder. Sam had been working in California for only a little over a month and a half and had just gotten his first check and now he was out of work. He was feeling angry at John again for not telling him that they would be snowed out for the winter when he asked him to come to California. He did not yell at him, though, feeling that there was no use because that was just the way that John was, and he should have know better. He also knew that he would still be alright, since they had been working ten hour days and six day weeks, he would have enough money with the two more checks he was going to get, to make the trip to New Mexico to be with his family, and with even enough money to rent a U-Haul trailer to take all of their belongs with him, but he had counted on having a lot more money saved before he left, but that was just not to be. So he set the few chokers that had to set before Mike called them into the landing and told them they were snowed out for the year even though there was still hardly an inch of snow on the ground at the time. After they unhooked the guy lines, Mike drove Sam and John to the cabin and on the way they passed the low-boy, the huge truck with the low trailer, on its way out to pick up the loader and then the Yarder. By the time they reached the cabin there was two inches of snow on the ground. Sam was only at the cabin long enough to pack up his cloths and say goodbye to John, who would stay in California. Then he was driving down out of the snowy mountains on his way to Crescent.

CHAPTER TWENTY
PORTLAND GOODBYE

Sam drove, away from the cabin, feeling very good about having some days off finally and going back to Oregon and Portland. Feeling very content he drove down out of the mountains along the narrow two-lane road that hugged the side of a steep mountain, with a rock wall on one side and a gigantic drop off on the other. Driving on the narrow road, with the very steep drop off, had him alert and concentrating on his driving. He got careless, though, and started driving too fast down the hill when a very sharp corner caught him by surprise. Fear gripped him as he squeezed the steering wheel tightly and then turned it sharply to the left, but the car still edged the steep drop off as it careened around the corner. There on the edge was some small gravel that had been thrown there by the cars going by, and when his tires hit the gravel that was lying on top of the paved road, the tires lost their traction and the car started sliding towards the edge like it was on a sheet of ice. Sam just knowing he was going over the edge did the only thing he thought he could do. As he continued to jam the steering wheel sharply to the left he gunned the engine and with Sam feeling that it was useless because both his back tires had to be off the road, and knowing for sure that he was about to fall off the road, and down the steep and long incline to his death, but to his great relief, the tires caught something, when he thought there could only be air to catch, and it let him go sliding around the corner and safety.

His heart was beating like a bass drum as he slowed way down and then stopped for a few minutes to settle himself, and wonder how the hell he had survived and how he could have been so careless. He continued then to drive slowly and very carefully down the rest of the mountain. Sam just could not understand why he was still alive. He knew the back of his car was off that ledge. He wondered if it was god who had saved him, but knew god would have no reason to do that, but then he thought maybe god didn't think he was such a bad guy as he thought he was, but he let it go, and continued to feel on edge all the way down the hill to Pine Grove before his nervousness finally left him.

He cashed his check at the one big supermarket in town, and then left the store finally feeling great with all that money in his pocket. His mood could not have been better as he drove slowly along the small town's main street looking at the all the people on the streets, and the colorful Christmas decorations in the store windows. As the street lights were flickering on in the twilight of the evening, big snow flakes started slowly floated from the sky and then melting on the warm hood of his little Nova. He couldn't help but think that it was such a beautiful Christmas scene looking almost like a Christmas card. He was feeling good also because he didn't have even one bill to pay with the big stack of beautiful twenties that he had locked up safely in his trunk, and he didn't even have to save it all because he still had his last check to come. The check that his Uncle Mike was going to mail to his folk's house, and it was bigger than the one he had just cashed. That last check would be more than enough for the trip he would be making to New Mexico to be with his family. He knew he had to see Cheryl before he left though. He wanted and needed to see her and say goodbye to her.

Sam stopped his car at a little barn-red tavern that appeared all by its lonely self far from any town in the midst of a forest of tall and wide, old growth pine trees that he was passing through on his way out of Northern California. He walked into the lonely tavern with its walls of rough redwood planks. There were only three people in the place, a couple who were sitting across a shiny surfaced, beautiful wood topped bar, from a bartender. Sam climbed into a stool close to the couple and said to the bartender, "Do you sell Coors here?"

"Yes do want a bottle?"

"I don't want to drink it here. I would like to buy five cases to go." The bartender surprised, said. "Five cases!" Calmly Sam said, "Yea, five cases. I'm on my way to Oregon and they don't sell it there. It's my favorite beer. I know that it's going to cost a lot to buy it here in a tavern, but I don't want to leave the interstate once I get on it except to buy gas until I get where I'm going. Have you got five cases to sell?"

"I've got some back in the cooler."

"Do you have five cases?"

"Let me go check." Sam followed him back to the cooler and was soon carrying three cases back to the bar. Three cases because that is all the bartender would sell him saving two for his regular customers. He pulled out one of the many twenty dollar bills from his billfold that he had just so recently received and paid the bartender. The couple was watching him with curiosity, and as he lifted the three cases to take them out to his car the young girl, turned around in her stool, and yelled. "Where's the party?" Sam looked around, smiled, and then said, jokingly, "In Oregon. Come on, I'll take you." The girl then pinched up her face, frowned, and said, "That's too far." Then she turned back to the bar, and Sam, while continuing to smile, walked out to his car to put his precious beer into the trunk and then continued on his way.

Sam traveled through Northern California on Interstate Five to Oregon and then on to Crescent. He stopped at his folks very late in the evening and stayed the night. The next day he called Cheryl about noon, after he had slept in very late, and told her he was coming to see her. Sam liked that she sounded happy to know he was coming, making him feel very good as he jumped in his car to make the trip. He arrived in Portland early that evening and then picked up Cheryl at Jackie's to go spend some of his money. It would be the first time that he had any real money when he took her out. Sam wanted them to really enjoy themselves on the last days they had together. The first thing he was going to do was take her out to eat a steak dinner. He had to convince her though because she wanted to just get fast food. She had always worried, from the time he first time met her, about him spending too much money on her. While they were driving to the restaurant, Cheryl said, "Sam, I was supposed to go to a party at Greg's house tonight. You remember Greg. Jackie's brother."

"Yea, he seems like a good guy."

"When I told Greg that I couldn't go because you were coming to see me, He told me to invite you. You don't have to go if you don't want to."

"Don't you want to go?"

"I'll go if you want to Sam. I really don't care." Sam was in the mood to party and do a little drinking after working the six day weeks and ten hour days in California for over a month and a half. "Let's go I think it will be fun. Cheryl was not only very good friends with her former sister-in-law, but with her entire family having lived with Jackie's parents at one time. Sam had meet Greg a few times and liked him. He was a big guy. He was fat but not all that fat. Very friendly and talkative, and he liked to drink and party. Cheryl told Sam that she would often go out with a group of his family and friends to play pool or bowl, and to party.

After they ate, Cheryl had Sam drive to a house a couple of blocks from Jackie's house. It was a big, old, two-story, wood frame, house in a line of houses, most of which were painted white. All the houses sat high above the street so their lawns were on a incline, and each old house had a large porch with big columns holding up their over hanging roofs, and each old porch had a very long, steep, stairway leading up to it. When Sam drove by the house to park he had to stop and park two houses down the street from it because of all the cars that lined both sides of the street. Sam said to Cheryl as he parking the car, "They must be having a hell of a party. Look at all those cars." Cheryl while staring at the many cars said, "Greg has a lot of friends and family."

"I guess so. Are you sure they're going to have room for us."

"It's a big house."

"It better be." Sam was feeling very good and getting a little excited and he hadn't even had a beer yet. He quickly jumped out of his car and yelled, "Let's go Cheryl! And party hearty." Cheryl didn't answer as she followed behind him taking long strides trying to catch up to him. Sam had already taken a white cross. He hadn't had one in a long time so it had quickly got him feeling good. As they continued walking up the street, Sam could see people standing on one of the porches drinking and talking making it very easy for him to spot the party house. When they reached the front door it was wide open so Sam and Cheryl walked right in. They then waded into a front room jammed with people sounding as loud as if all of them were talking at once. Greg yelled Cheryl's name, over the din, and then the big man came pushing through the crowd to where she and Sam were standing surrounded by partiers. "Cher! It's good to see you." Then he turned to Sam and held out his hand for him to shake, "I'm glad that you could make it Sam. You don't have a beer. Why don't you go back in the kitchen? There is a case of beer on the table." Sam smiled broadly and said. "Why, thanks, Greg, I could use a beer." He knew he could use many beers being that he wanted to finally get drunk and was at a party where he knew practically no one. He then, raising his voice over the din, asked, "Cheryl, do you want a beer?"

"Of course, do you have to ask?"

"Oh yeah, I forgot how much you love to drink."

"Sam! Don't let everyone know."

"I thought everyone knew already." Sam then smiled a little smile at Cheryl and as she returned the smile, he turned and left her and Greg standing there and went on into the kitchen to grab a couple of cans of beer. Pulling the tab off one, he took a long thirsty swallow. The beer tasted so good to him after not having one for over a month. He then walked back to the front room. Cheryl was standing there talking to a couple of girls and she introduced them to Sam as he handed her the beer. Then she walked with him around the room introducing him to more of the crowd. Everyone seemed to want to talk to Cheryl, and as they gathered around her she would entertain them with her quick wit and self-depreciating humor. She so often made fun of herself, to get a laugh and she was good at it. Staring at her talking to her friends Sam had a strange thought that she was like a little stray puppy caught in a rain storm, which with its hair slicked down by the rain, looked so lonely that you could not help but stop, pick up the puppy and take it home to wrap in a blanket and put it by a warm stove. Cheryl was popular at the party, but not Sam who, late in the party, had only talked to Greg the one time, and except for some introductions no one else. Not that he hadn't tried, but no one seemed to want to talk to poor Sam. Greg had a group of friends who he would talk to most of the time ignoring Sam. Sam was feeling out of place, but he contented himself with drinking a lot of beer which he didn't feel was so bad a deal, but it was not quite the party he thought it would be for him. Cheryl would check on him every now and then to see if he was doing all right. Most of the time she would find him by himself sitting in the front room in an easy chair, steadily emptying cans of beer. He wondered as he sat there in that chair if these friends of Cheryl might be snubbing him because they didn't like that he was seeing Cheryl. Since he was a married man. He eventually felt that had to be the reason and that he should have known how her friends were going to act and not come to the party. Cheryl had not seemed to really want to come to the party maybe she knew how it would be. He knew that if her friends did feel that way. He could not blame them, but it made for a lonely night for him. After awhile a young man who was way over weight and with a bad case of acne did come over to talk with him as he was sitting in his chair feeling sorry for himself. He said, "Hi, Sam." Sam looked up at him from his chair for a second and then said sounding a little drunk, "Hi! How you doing?"

"I'm a friend of Cheryl's. You met when you first came in."

"Oh, yea. Your names Herb right?"

"Yes, that's me. Cheryl says you work in the woods. I bet that's hard work."

"Yes it is. Dangerous too."

"Really? Have you had any close calls?"

"A choker setter I was working with got hit in the mouth with a steel cable the other day."

"How bad was he hurt?"

"He was very lucky. He didn't get hit very badly. He ended up with a bloody nose and some broken teeth. He could have easily been killed."

"Wow, I know that I'll never work in the woods."

"It's not so bad if you know what you're doing out there." Sam tipped his head back and lifted his beer to his mouth, and then guzzled the last of the beer in it before excusing himself and going to look for another beer. There was no beer left though, and Sam knew he was guilty of drinking a lot of it much more than he should have. He really wanted to keep drinking so as he stood there staring at the empty case of beer he remembered the three cases of Coors that he had in the trunk of his car. He quickly went looking for Greg and found him still holding court with his friends. As Sam approached he said, a little too loudly because he was definitely feeling his beer, "Hey! Greg, you're out of beer. It's not much of a party without beer. I've got three cases of Coors beer that I brought from California. I could bring in a case if you want. I would still have two cases for myself."

"Sam, I can't let you do that. You bought that Coors for yourself. I like Coor's to but it's your's."

"It's alright. I can spare a case. I want you to have it for your party. I drank a lot of your beer. I would just be paying you back." Sam had thought that he was doing such a cool thing and could not believe that Greg did not want him bring the beer in. Sam wanted a beer bad, though, so he asked, "Greg, I really need a beer, you mind if I bring a few in for myself?"

"Sure, Sam, Go ahead bring in a few for yourself." Then Sam, staggering a little, walked to the front door. He knew he was getting drunker by the minute and did not need another beer but drunk as he was he was still determined to keep drinking. He had gone through a lot for the last month and a half. He had worked very hard sometimes all seven days of the week. He deserved to get good and drunk. He knew that he should not have used Greg's party to do it, but he had and it was done and he was drunk. Cheryl had seen him stagger so she followed him out to his car and while he was opening the trunk she said, "Sam, you shouldn't drink any more beer you're drunk." Sam, surprised, looked around to see Cheryl standing there and not looking very happy. Leaning against the back of the car for support, he said, "Naw! Cheryl I'm not even near drunk." Then, instead of a few beers, he pulled a whole case out of the trunk. Lifting it onto his shoulder he started walking across the street saying to Cheryl. "I'm as sober as a church mouse." He then took his treasure into the house, ignoring Cheryl as he walked by her, and deposited it on the kitchen table. There he tore open the cardboard covering and lifted out a six pack. After he pulled a beer out of the plastic rings he put the others into the refrigerator. Then he went into the living room carrying an already half-empty can of beer. A lot of the crowd was gone by then as the party was finally winding down. The way Sam was feeling the party was finally getting good. He was having a little trouble walking straight, but he was feeling fine. He walked up to Cheryl, who was talking to two girls who so closely resembled each other Sam thought they had to be sisters, and said loudly, interrupting them, "Well, how are you beautiful girls doing?" Then he put his arm around Cheryl and kissed her on the cheek. He backed away from her, though, when she didn't turn to look at him. Seeing how drunk and loud he was the two girls looked at him with a little fear in their eyes as he turned to them and said, "Great party, huh, girls?" They both quickly said in unison, "Yes, it is." Cheryl, realizing that Sam was not going away, said, "I think you girls have met Sam before?" One of the girls said. "Hi, Sam."

"Well, hello pretty girl." Sam lifted his beer to his mouth finishing the last of the beer that was in it. "Excuse me, ladies. I seemed to have finished the last of my beer and need to get another." He then turned and walked unsteadily to the kitchen door. After he walked into the kitchen he was shocked to find that all the beer that he had left on the table was gone. He quickly looked in the refrigerator to see the beer that he had put in there was also gone. He closed the refrigerator door and yelled. "What happened to my beer? Someone has stolen my beer. Dammit where is my beer?" He rushed back into the living room to see everyone there staring at him as he entered. He turned to Greg and said, "Greg someone has stolen my beer. Do you know what happened to it? Did you put it somewhere?" "Sam, I haven't been in the kitchen since you took it in there. I don't know what happened to it." Greg went into the kitchen with Sam, Cheryl following him in. Greg looked around the kitchen and in a large pantry, then went back into the living room and asked everyone there if they had seen what happened to Sam's beer. No one said a thing so he turned to Sam and said, "There have been a lot of people at this party and some of them I don't even know, anyone of them could have taken it." He put his arm around Sam and said, "I'm sorry Sam, but it's gone. It must have gone out the back door. I or someone would have seen it if had been taken out the front door. You can go look out on the deck and the back yard to see if someone has stashed it out there if you want, but I think it is long gone. Sam could tell, by the way he acted, that Greg did not want to bother with his missing beer anymore so he just said, "Okay I'll check it out." He was also sure by then that he would not find it. He knew that it had to be long gone or hidden somewhere, but he went out on the back deck anyway. It was a very large and usual deck. It was high off the ground and had a walkway that led to a house that sat very close behind Greg's house and walkway to the house next door. It was like a community deck. There was no beer to be found, though, just as he had thought, not that he looked very hard for it though. Cheryl soon followed him out onto the deck and as they sat on a rough wooden bench, with Sam sitting very dejectedly, Cheryl said softly, "Sam, you don't need anymore beer." Staring at the ground he said. "I know, but I don't like people stealing from me."

"I know Sam, but maybe it's a good thing that you don't have anymore beer to drink." Sam then began to think that maybe it was Cheryl who was behind the disappearing beer by having it hid, or hiding it to stop him from drinking any more. He quickly let that thought pass though because he was mad, and he wanted to stay mad, and he could not stay mad at Cheryl for very long, or want her to get mad at him. Sam stood up abruptly and said, "Are you ready to go?" I want to leave." Cheryl then got up with Sam and said. "Okay Sam, Let's go, if you want to." He then walked angrily through the kitchen and into the front room while staring straight ahead and not saying not a word to anyone, and then out the open front door. Cheryl followed him, but stopped in the front room to say goodbye to her friends. Sam waited for her on the front porch getting angrier and more paranoid by the minute. She hurried her goodbyes, knowing he was waiting for her, so it wasn't long before she was out on the porch with him. Greg and a couple of the other partygoers followed her out onto the porch. Greg put out his hand to shake Sam's and said. It was good to see you Sam. I'm sorry about you're beer." Sam, who was still steaming, and so very drunk, said angrily, "I think you or one of your friends took my beer." Cheryl immediately screamed, "Sam! Greg is my friend he would not steal your beer." She grabbed his arm and pulled him down the stairs almost making him fall as she did. Sam resisted her pull at the bottom of the stairs so they stopped. He then looked up at the porch which was filled with people and yelled, angrily, "You sons of bitches. I know you took my beer!" Greg called down to him calmly, "Sam we would never take your beer. What did you pay for it? I'll give you whatever you paid for it."

"I don't want your money, I want my beer asshole." Cheryl started pulling on his arm again. He resisted but in his drunken state, and with her determination, he could not keep her from pulling him out to the front gate. At the gate Sam yelled again, "I ought to kick your asses." Cheryl then pulled him into the street where she said to him, "Sam, shut up! You're not going to fight anyone. We're leaving." Sam had began thinking that Greg and his boys had been patronizing him, treating like his was some dumb wimp, so when Cheryl had him almost pulled to the car he pulled loose from her, which was not easy as drunk as he was. He then started staggering back across the street yelling as he went. "You son's a bitches. I'm going to kick your asses!" Cheryl was on him like a flash pulling him back across the street by his arm. Sam was having a hard time trying to pull away from her as drunk as he was. He knew she was strong for a woman but he could hot believe how tightly she held him. It took all his might to break away from her. Just as soon as he did, and before he could get to the other side of the street, she had his arm again and was pulling him back. They went back and forth like that many times giving the people on the porch quite a show, with Sam getting loose and staggering across the street to try to confront his enemies and then Cheryl chasing him down and pulling him back. Sam was very frustrated but knew that he would never hit her to get away from her, and knowing there was no other way as drunk as he was that he could get away from her. He wanted so badly to get away that he started pleading with her to let go of him, but she would not listen. After many trips back and forth across the street, Sam had spent all of his anger and finally stopped trying to get away from Cheryl. He calmly told her as both of them stood in the middle of the street bent over and breathing heavily from their exertions. "Okay, Cheryl I give up. Let's go." They then drove off, with the crowd still watching from the porch as Sam's car disappeared down the street. They were both so tired that Sam stopped at the first motel they came to and rented a room for the night. They could not sleep until they made love though. Very soon after that they fell soundly asleep and slept until late the next morning.

When they woke the first thing they did was make love again. Then they were off to have breakfast. When they got to the restaurant the first thing Sam had to do was to get some of his twenties out of his trunk, and then as he sat there in the restaurant eating his ham and eggs, looking across the table at Cheryl he wondered how he was going to tell her that he would be leaving for New Mexico in a week. He knew that he had already told her that he was going back to Brenda and Patrick, but he also knew that she hadn't really believed him. It had been so long since Brenda had left, and he had told her that he loved her so many times since that time, and had visited her almost every weekend after Brenda left when she wasn't with him in Crescent or he was in California, and he had never really shown her any real urgency that he was making the trip, and she knew he was spending most of his money on her until he went to California. He knew that since he had not acted like he was leaving her that she had every reason to believe that he would never leave her, but he was. It had been awhile since he decided he was going back to his family, and there were times when even he wavered and did not believe he was ever going to be able to make the trip since he had been unable to save any money for the trip until the job in California. He knew he could have and should have made it plainer that he was really going to go back to his family, but he knew the only way he could do that was to quit seeing her and he had not been able to do that.

Cheryl wanted to see Jackie, so after they ate their breakfast Sam drove her to Jackie's house. Jackie, still in her housecoat at eleven thirty in the morning, had already heard about what happened the night before at her brother's party. So the first thing that she said as she met them at the front door was, "I heard that was some party you had last night." Cheryl answered her by simply saying, "Sam got a little drunk."

"Yes. I heard. How's your head this morning Sam?"

"It's not feeling too good."

"I'll bet it isn't." Sam looking contrite said. "I really am sorry for how stupid I acted last night. I was very drunk and didn't know what I was doing or saying. When you see Greg, tell him I'm sorry."

"I heard it was you and Cheryl who were fighting last night" Sam laughed at that and said, "Yea she kicked my ass. This girl is very strong or I'm very weak. I could not get away from her." Cheryl said quickly, "Sam you were so drunk you could hardly walk." He turned to her and said seriously, "Cheryl you do have a strong grip." Cheryl flexing her arms said, "Yea, I'm like "The Claw" that wrestler." Sandy smiled, and looking at Cheryl quickly quipped, "I heard you were quite a wrestler Cheryl."

"Shut up, Jackie or I will tell Sam what you do for a living." All three of them laughed at that and then Cheryl said, "Jackie, Sam and I are going to pick up some whites, do you want any?"

"No, I don't have any money right now. I wish I could but I can't," Then Cheryl said, "Well, we're going over there now. I'll bring you some of mine."

"See you guys later, then, and drive safe." Sam and Cheryl then walked down off the porch and drove off. After they had driven about a block Sam turned to Cheryl and said, "We're going to get some whites?"

Cheryl pretending to look shocked said, "Oh! Didn't I tell you that we were going to get some whites?"

"No, you didn't tell me," Cheryl put her arm around Sam and said sweetly, "You want to get some, don't you Sam?" Sam looking stern, said, "Do you have any money?"

"No, but I know that you like them, and thought if you bought some we could share them."

"Okay, three quarters of the pills for me and a quarter for you."

"Now you're getting greedy Sam."

"Well, I can't be greedy. We'll split then, half for you half for me."

"Sam, you're a doll."

"I know it." Cheryl had Sam drive to where he had waited for her to buy the whites before. He parked again by the large open field across from the long row of small white houses. After Sam gave her the money Cheryl walked off towards the houses like she had done before and fear again nagged Sam. He again was checking out his rear view mirror, and feeling like a fugitive from some television show as he sat there worried and anxious feeling that he should stop taking the little pills. He knew, though, that except for when he was doing what he was doing then, he never worried about using them or having them on him, and he knew that the way that he was getting used to them that he would want to find his own provider once he moved to New Mexico. So he had better get used to what he and Cheryl were doing. As he sat there and tried to relax he remembered the night he and Cheryl had gone to Cheryl's friend Katy's house, there in Portland, a couple of months earlier. Katy had looked and acted so differently, Sam thought, than when he had shown her and Cheryl around the University of Oregon Campus.

She was much thinner with her face gaunt and her hair cut much shorter almost in a buzz cut. Sam thought she had lost her good looks although he knew they were some who would think she looked better.

She had been getting ready for work when they stopped by. She was working at a night club then serving drinks and was wearing her work cloths a leather, mini dress and vest. Sam, looking at her, thought that the way she was dressed she was bound to get a lot of tips. As they waited for Katy to finish getting ready Sam's attention was caught by the couple that was sitting on the floor in her living room. At first Sam thought that they were watching television but the television wasn't on, and as he watched them they did not move an inch, looking like statues, the whole time that he and Cheryl were there. Katy acted as if they weren't even there; walking around them as they stared like zombies, so eerily, at a blank television screen, after they left Cheryl told him that Katy had told her that the couple had been taking heroin. Sam then quickly told Cheryl that they had to be crazy to be taking a drug that would make them act like that. The little white crosses that he took never make him act like that. He knew they were uppers though not a downer like heroin, but he remembered what Cheryl had told him about her friend who had to take more and more of them to feel good and ended up getting addicted to them. Sam had also started seeing news stories about amphetamines on television and was also learning more about them from reading stories in the Eugene newspaper. Stories of people getting arrested for possessing them, and even stories of people in little Crescent getting arrested for having labs where they made the stuff. It worried him when he learned that people who took a lot of them could end up with paranoia, psychosis, and end up possibly having a stroke. It worried Sam but not enough for him to stop using them after all he thought he was still only taking one at a time.

Cheryl finally came back to the car. Sam relieved because they could leave the area. After they had driven a few miles, Sam became more comfortable even though they now had the amphetamines in their possession. Cheryl had the pills in a plastic sandwich bag. She took another sandwich bag out of her purse and divided the pills into the two bags, and then she gave Sam one of the bags. Sam stopped at a small Convience store and bought a coke then he drove to a city park. After Sam parked the car, they each swallowed a pill and washed them down with the coke. Cheryl scooted up close to Sam and he put his arm around her. Then he said, as they sat there quietly viewing the greenery in front of them, "Cheryl you know that I love you?" She turned quickly to look at him, and after studying his face a little she smiled and said, "You're not going to get mushy on me now. Are you Sam?" Sam didn't smile like he would have anytime before that day. This time he turned to her and said, very seriously, "I'm going back to Brenda and Patrick." Cheryl a little shocked at his abruptness, said nothing but after a few seconds she said,

"I know you want to go back to your wife and little boy. You have told me before and I know someday you will."

"I am going soon." Cheryl now very serious said, "How soon?"

"Sometime next week. They're mailing my last check from California to my Mom's house. It's a big check. A big enough check for me to make the trip to New Mexico towing a u-haul trailer." Cheryl sat there quietly, not saying a word, staring ahead at nothing. Sam, feeling bad, waited for her to speak and eventually she did say, "Sam, I know that you have to go back to you family and you should."

"Cheryl, I don't want to leave you, you know that, but I want to raise my son, and I should raise him." Sam then sat there quietly feeling bad when Cheryl said, "Can you take me along? I don't take up much room." Sam smiled, knowing again why he loved her. The mood of the car had suddenly lightened causing Sam to smile broadly, and say, "Yea! We could trade off driving so we could get there faster."

"I always wanted to be your kept woman."

"I'm rich now I could afford to keep you in style. I have all that money in my trunk." Sam getting serious again, said, "How I wish I was really rich Cheryl. I would keep you in the most expensive apartment in town, and I would." The car was quiet for awhile before Sam started the car and happily raising his voice. Let's go get a motel room and then go out and party. I feel like dancing lets go to a club."

"Yes, if you've got the money I sure have the time." Sam found a motel that looked like it would not be too expensive, and then he turned in and jerked his car to a stop in a parking place close the motel office. He walked quickly into the glassed in office. There was no one in the small sparsely furnished office so Sam rang a little bell they had sitting on the counter. A short, thin, red headed, young man, with thick glasses, rushed out of a back room, and looking like he was being put out said hurriedly. Can I help you?" Sam almost didn't answer him because of his attitude but said, "I need a room for me and my wife."

"We don't have any single rooms left, because of a convention, but we have some of the larger rooms left the ones with kitchens and separate bedrooms."

"I don't want a room that big."

"I can let you have it for the price of a single room."

"How much is that?"

"Thirty six dollars a night."

"I'll take it then." So Sam handed him the money in exchange for the keys. Then he and Cheryl walked up a stairway to a second story room. Inside Sam looked around a big front room said to Cheryl. "They didn't have any regular sized rooms, but the clerk let us have this large room for the same price as the smaller room."

"Well this room certainly is big. I've never seen a motel room this big."

"Oh! You've stayed in a lot of motel rooms?"

"Wouldn't you like to know, big boy." Sam laughed and said, "There is even supposed to be a kitchen somewhere. It must be though that hallway. Sam walked through the hallway and into the kitchen with Cheryl right behind him. After looking around the kitchen Sam said, "Wow! This kitchen is bigger than the one I had in my apartment. I bet this place is bigger than my apartment."

"I know why you got this place Sam. You want me to cook dinner for you." Sam laughed and said, "Yep, You guessed it. I'm just about ready to go get some groceries."

"Sorry, Sam, no utensils or pots and pans."

"Dang. My plan is foiled." Then walking out of the kitchen and Sam said, "There is also has to be a bedroom somewhere." At the far end of a long front room they found the entry to the bedroom and once they walked in Sam said, "This is the room I've been looking for. Do you know why?"

"I think I have a good idea why." Sam put his arm around her and she looked up at him and said, "I was right." Sam laughed then and kissed Cheryl a long lip-smashing kiss before he laid her slowly down on the bed. There they made love with power, passion, and abandon and afterwards they lay there wrapped together, totally spent, resting and enjoying the moment, and then they lay back and took a nap resting for the evening. Eventually Cheryl got up and showered and then Sam did the same. They dressed and both of them swallowed another of their little white energy pills before they left and drove off to one of their favorite places. It was a Chinese restaurant and bar named "Chopsticks." It had live music and dancing every night of the week. Sam and Cheryl had been there many times and really like it. Sam drove into the big parking lot by the restaurant. A large red neon sign, with a black dragon painted on it stood out in front of the long wood sided building that was painted red and topped by a green, oriental, decorative roof. After parking his car, Sam opened the trunk, and after looking around and seeing no one. He took some of his cache of dwindling twenty-dollar bills. Entering "Chopsticks," Sam and Cheryl faced a long room filled to the brim with tables and people. At the far end of the room, in front of a small dance floor crowded with dancers, was a band blaring county music. The place was so crowded that Sam had a hard time finding a place for him and Cheryl to sit. Luckily he found a place in the back far away from the blaring band. He and Cheryl sat quickly down so no one would steal their seats and Sam order two beers. Because of the good service of the barmaids, they were constantly hovering near by; they were able to drink a lot of beer very fast, which is exactly what they both wanted to do, so they were soon feeling extremely good. That night they were much more serious about their drinking than they usually were when they were at Chopsticks, and not as happy. They spent over four hours, drinking, dancing, and getting drunk. They finally had to leave because they had gotten so drunk that it was impossible for them to dance. When they got outside, they had to hold each other for support as they staggered through the parking lot, zig-zagging their way back to the car. Sam drove his car very slowly and carefully back to the motel, but still hit a couple of curbs. They were very lucky not to run into a policeman or Sam would have been stopped for going too slow and weaving, and then he would have really been in trouble. When they got to the motel they fell into bed together, too tired and too drunk to even try to make love.

The next morning Sam woke to a humongous headache and Cheryl did not feel much better than he did. They were more than willing, though, to make up for not making love the night before. Later on, they left the motel to eat a very late breakfast, at a fast food restaurant, and then Sam drove Cheryl to Jackie's so he could drive back to Crescent. He told her there that he would be back by the end of the week, to see her, before he left for New Mexico. As Sam told her she said nothing. Sam still felt as he left for Crescent, that Cheryl still did not believe that he was leaving. He had made up his mind and had the money now. He loved her and even though he loved her, and even with their long distance life together he was leaving.

Chapter Twenty-One
Sam Leaves

Sam waited four whole days at his folk's house waiting for his last paycheck from California. The time did give him time to rent, and load a u-haul trailer for his trip to New Mexico. His folks were happy to have him there, especially his mother. She had one of her chick's come home so that she could mother-hen him. Thursday his check finally showed up in the mail. He cashed it, made his good byes to his family, and was quickly off on his way to Portland. He felt good like he always did when he was driving to Portland to see Cheryl, but this time it was very different. It was the last time that he would see her so there was sadness also. That was something that had never traveled with him before on his trips to Portland.

He drove up to Jackie's house and, as he walked towards the porch, Cheryl, who had been watching for him, walked out of the house to greet him. Neither of them showed much happiness as they made their way to Sam's car and drove off. Cheryl saw the suit cases in the backseat of Sam' car, and knew absolutely then that Sam was leaving. So she said accusingly, "It looks like you're all packed up and ready to go?"

I'm leaving from here. I'm just going to stop in Crescent long enough to hook up a u-haul trailer. "I said goodbye to my mother and step-father before I left to see you." Sam drove to a city park they often visited. After he stopped Cheryl scooted over next to him. He was a little worried that she would not, but she was snuggled tightly up against yet feeling so soft. They sat there for awhile feeling each others pain. Then Sam turned to Cheryl and said, "Cheryl you know that I will love you forever. I will always miss you and you will always be a part of me."

"If you believe that, then why are you leaving me?"

"I have to especially for my son's sake.

Cheryl most of the time acted as if she was so very tough, immune to life's buffeting, although she experienced a lot of it, and always talking so big and joking around. Acting like she could not be hurt or affected by what people said or did. Sam was always able to see her soft side, though, the side that she always tried to cover up, and what he could see in her then. She did not like to be vulnerable especially to show that vulnerability to anyone else, even Sam. She had fallen in love with Sam, though, and stayed in love with him even after the things he had done to her, and knowing how weak he could be. She didn't even care that he was married. She had trusted that his love for her would not let him leave her, no matter what he said, and now he was truly leaving her, hurting her like he had done before. Just like her ex husband and other people in her life had done. She sat there beside Sam feeling so alone and feeling that she would never learn. Sam, sensing the way she was feeling, said, "Cheryl, being with you has given me the best times of my life, and I am so sorry. You have become a part of me. I will carry you in my heart forever." Cheryl loved for Sam to say things like that to her, and always thought he was sincere, though her tough side thought it mushy. Now he was leaving her, not to be gone for a week. But he was leaving her to be gone forever. She knew he would soon be taking her back to Sandy's and then he would drive down the street and out of her life. She would not cry in front of him and show him how much he was hurting her. So, turning to him she said, "Sam, we had some good times and we had some bad times, and you know what those times were." Feeling very guilty Sam said, "Yes Cheryl I know what I did. Cheryl, feeling so hurt then, and so mad that he was leaving her, just wanted to get away from him. She didn't know if she wanted to cry or yell or kick Sam where it would hurt him the most, but she knew she had to leave him before she lost control, so she quickly said, "Sam, I just want to go back to Sandy's" Sam, hearing the tenseness in her voice and knowing there was absolutely nothing he could say that would help her feel better, started his car and drove out of the park. Cheryl continued to sit beside him, but her body stiffened and her gaze was set firmly ahead. Sam, sitting there, feeling guiltier by the minute, drove on towards Sandy's house. He ached to hold her, but knew that he could not. Neither of them said a thing until they got to Sandy's house where Cheryl let Sam kiss her and hold her tight before he again told he loved her. She then got out of his car and he drove away. Sam had to turn around to watch Cheryl walk down the sidewalk away from him trying to take a picture of her with his mind that would have to last forever. She entered the house and then Sam turned quickly back to watch the road. Driving slowly through Portland he felt drained and so lonely knowing he would never see Cheryl again. Overhead, the sky was a dark gray, fitting his mood, and it was starting to lightly rain on his windshield so he turned on the wipers. It turned even darker and rained even harder as he drove south by Salem. While he drove on he took out the small plastic prescription bottle that he had put his white crosses in. Since it was a very long drive he knew the little pills would help him. They would give him energy when he got tired of driving, and keep him awake when he drove at night. He was going to try to drive all the way without stopping if he could.

As he held the little plastic bottle in his hand, he thought of the brand new life that he had ahead of him in New Mexico, and knew he did not want the pills to be controlling him in that new life. If he was to do anything in his life he wanted to do it on his own not with the help of pills. He was doing what was right finally. He was going back to his wife and child. He had a new start in life and he was going to make the best of it. He rolled down his window, as he passed a rest area, and stuck his arm out in the rain and then heaved the little bottle. Then he smiled to himself, knowing he had done the right thing. Out on the rain slicked highway, the bottle bounced on the road behind Sam's car breaking open and spilling little white pills all over the damp, black, road.

The drive was long and tiring, but the closer he got to his family the better he felt. He was really looking forward to another chance in life and his marriage, and to prove all over again to his wife that he loved her. He knew he would never go through another night like the night when he told her he wanted to leave her. It was the worst night of his life, and he promised himself that he would never, ever, make him or her go through that again. In a little county town in New Mexico there was a wonderful reunion when Sam drove his little Nova up to the front of Brenda's parent's house starting their new life.

THE END